RENDEZVOUS WITH LOVE

Can the deep love between Roz Henson and Max Pierce survive the unbelievable test to which it is to be put? Their wedding is arranged and then, out of Max's past, Sybille Klein arrives in England, and it seems that the police know every detail about the few months he spent in Germany, and his love affair with the beautiful German girl. Then Sybille is caught spying. She says it was to save her mother who is still behind the Iron Curtain. So she returns home, her mission complete — or is it?

JUDY CHARD

◆

RENDEZVOUS WITH LOVE

Complete and Unabridged

LINFORD
Leicester

First published in Great Britain in 1983

First Linford Edition
published 2004

British Library CIP Data

Chard, Judy
    Rendezvous with love.—Large print ed.—
    Linford romance library
    1. Love stories
    2. Large type books
    I. Title
    823.9'14 [F]

    ISBN 1–84395–416–8

Published by
F. A. Thorpe (Publishing)
Anstey, Leicestershire

Set by Words & Graphics Ltd.
Anstey, Leicestershire
Printed and bound in Great Britain by
T. J. International Ltd., Padstow, Cornwall

This book is printed on acid-free paper

1

The back door stood open to the fields, the girl came in wearing a torn shirt and a pair of men's old cord trousers with a large patch on the rear. Her skin was turned to honey by the sun, her hair corn-gold, she looked like a blonde gipsy.

The man held out his arms and she went into them with a little sigh of content.

'You've got scarlet paint on your nose, and we're not painting anything scarlet.' He nuzzled her neck as he spoke.

'I know, but I was cleaning some old brushes and it dropped into the spirit.' She lifted her head and glanced over his shoulder to the table where the pots of paint and jam jars of cleaning spirit stood. 'What you don't know is that you've just put your brush with the non-drip-high-gloss-unchippable, ever-lasting gunge into your coffee mug and we hadn't bargained for that on our ceiling. We planned on cream, remember, not the Michaelangelo 'fresco bit'.'

He pulled her tighter to him, covering her lips with his. 'Who cares,' he murmured. 'It's you I shall be gazing at during breakfast, not the ceiling.'

She drew away. 'Max, the workmen are only across the hall!'

'Don't go prissy on me, Rosalind — they are human — actually I saw Pat, the foreman, giving you a very old-fashioned look from one of the upstairs windows last week when you were digging the vegetable patch in those shorts of yours.'

'Good, you're jealous — and they're Bermudas.'

She flung herself down in the wide window seat; behind her, like a backcloth stretched the fields and woods of the manor on whose estate stood the cottage which they had bought. They got it cheap because the

Lord of the Manor needed the cash for his string of racehorses which seemed to have a habit of being last past the post, and because there was a lot of work to be done to make it habitable. Only people with vision and some money to spend would have undertaken it, certainly no Building Society would have advanced anything on such a project. It had been the gardener's cottage originally, stone built with a slate roof, and windows lozenged with lead. Roz had fallen in love with it as soon as she saw it.

'Oh, Max, this is it, our home, our nest — please, we must have it!'

'Darling, you are so romantic, you will let your heart rule your head. It's probably riddled with woodworm and we shall be able to lie in bed and listen to the tattoo of the death watch beetle as it calls to its mate.'

They had sat in his scarlet sports car in the drive, looking at it. It was autumn, the garden a tangle of shoulder high weeds with leaning stacks of withered Michaelmas daisies choked by dragging tendrils of convolvulus.

Roz had worked all through the winter months and early spring, digging, pruning, giving little exclamations of delight as she found a new treasure; a clump of Christmas roses, an old fashioned sweet smelling rose, a climbing Albertine; running into the house to fetch Max.

'You must come and see this!'

With a sigh of resignation he had put down whatever he had been doing and followed her into the garden to see her latest find, but in the end he had to admit he, too, had succumbed to the enchantment, the almost magic spell of the little house and garden.

'You know, Max, people have been happy here; you can tell at once. A house has an atmosphere, a kind of charisma like a person. What was it Kipling called it? Feng shui — the spirits of the house, and these are definitely friendly.'

His lips rested on her hair, which had

its own delightful fragrance, a freshness that always seemed to hang around her.

'For an intellectual, highly-trained radiologist with degrees and I don't know what, you seem to have a very romantic side to you. Maybe that's why I love you like I do.'

She turned round within the circle of his arms, looking up at him, wide-eyed, so that he could see himself reflected in the pupils; surrounded by a colour that reminded him of the sea, almost emerald, and yet at times, if her emotions were aroused, they were dark blue, inscrutable. Sometimes he couldn't believe his luck in having met her, in the fact that she actually loved him . . . that they were to be married . . . Now he flopped down beside her in the window seat.

'Darned hard work, painting ceilings. I always thought Michaelangelo had a doddle . . . '

She touched the end of his nose with her finger. 'Tell you what, I think you ought just to check with the plumber in the bathroom, he seemed to be having a problem. It's the pressure, apparently; as it's a well the water comes from there's something to do with the gravity feed. It sounded all very technical, I suppose really we should have had the bathroom downstairs, but that little room at the end of the passage seemed just right.'

He stood up. 'OK, boss, I'll go and give my expert opinion, of which, having listened with great attention, the powers that be will take not the slightest notice.' He grinned and ruffled her already tousled hair. 'I love your hair like that; must you put it up in that bun thing?'

She burst out laughing. 'That 'bun thing' is a very trendy French pleat, I'll have you know, which took me months to master, and really, darling, I can't see me swanning about in the hospital wards with hair trailing all round my collar — most unhygienic!' She gave a little sniff.

'I love you when you're all professional, just another side to your personality.' He turned and went out of the kitchen. 'See you when I've dealt with this water problem. You could make yourself useful meanwhile by brewing up another cup of coffee since I seem to have had a slight accident with mine.'

Grinning to herself, she got up and lighted the little bottled gas ring they had brought with them, singing softly as she did so. As she watched the kettle boil she thought how lucky she was — Max was everything she had always dreamed of in a man, even to his looks, which she had heard described as dishy by the girls in reception at the hospital when he had come to call for her.

At thirty-two he was, in her opinion, and obviously of others, too, one of the most attractive men she had ever known, and in her job she had the chance to observe and to assess what made both men and women attractive — and the opposite — under the most trying conditions, too, of illness, anxiety and fear. He had naturally blond hair that had turned darker — a richer, more streaky gold as he grew older. He had what she called 'Viking eyes', as blue as if they reflected summer skies. They closed almost when he smiled so that the little lines at the corner deepened, making him look somehow wise but merry at the same time. His nose was straight and one front tooth was chipped which gave him an endearing small boy look, making her want to cuddle him the first moment she had seen him.

She gave an involuntary sigh, part happiness part desire, for although their love making was passionate and in a way, expert, they had not slept together, by mutual consent wanting to wait for the culmination of their love when they were married — and that was two months away.

They had chosen August because the firm preferred their employees to take the largest section of their vacation then when so many business premises were closed anyway — Max worked for Roz's father — Edward Henson, and although he may have laughingly referred to her own intellect, he himself was, she knew, quite a brilliant electronics engineer.

Her father's firm had started in a small way, but some years ago they had gone into the laser side of the business. Roz knew some of the technicalities herself so that they could discuss developments, and she knew a whole new wide world was opening up — medical, as well as in the video field where laser discs were going to be the newest development for recording both sound and vision.

'Things move so fast in the electronics field nowadays — I suppose in most other fields as well for that matter — but this is the one I know — every day you learn something fresh, and you need to keep up with the world demand.' Max had told her that only yesterday, his face serious. She had put her hand over his across the table in the restaurant where they were dining.

'Obviously you don't have much trouble in that direction, I know Dad thinks the world of you — he never says so, of course, with real Midland determination that you shan't get 'uppity', like all his other associates.'

Max had thrown back his head and roared with laughter.

'What a perfect word, a marvellous description of some of the folk I know, don't we all. I must remember that,' he wagged his finger at her, 'and don't you get uppity yourself, young woman.'

The kettle boiled over and brought her back to reality. Quickly she turned off the gas and poured water on the grounds, the fragrance tickling her nostrils.

'Lovely!' Max said from the doorway. 'Just what I need after talking to Plumber Plod.' He took the mug from her, sniffing at the liquid. 'Funny thing, often the anticipation of something is better than the realisation; there's a profound thought for you.' His wide grin belied the seriousness of the remark.

She shrugged. 'Sometimes.' She paused a moment and then looked at him. 'You don't think that refers to marriage, do you?'

He put his arm along her shoulders. 'No, not in our case. It may in some, but we've known each other a long time, we're mature people. I think it should work.'

She gave him a quick glance, not sure now if he were serious or being light-hearted. But he had turned away and taken up his paint brush again so she couldn't see the expression in his eyes.

She put down her mug, stretched her arms above her head. 'Well, I'm on the crest of a wave, as someone used to sing, so won't you join me Mr Pierce, sir?'

He balanced the paint pot precariously on the top of the steps. 'Don't distract me, woman, I'm on man's work here and need no interruptions.'

She took a piece of paper from her pocket. 'Well, since painting only takes a little concentration and not much actual thought, I'll read out the list of wedding guests and you can add anyone I may have missed.'

'Good lord, surely we don't need to do that yet?'

'Look love, you know how the days fly, and I'm pretty tied up at the hospital, there isn't all that much time, and I'll have to find someone to take on the flat — I know it shouldn't be difficult, but Mrs Milton, my landlady, has always been a poppet to me and I don't want to land her with just anyone. And it all takes time.'

Max could never quite understand why Roz had chosen to live in a flat when she could have lived in the family home with her father, who was a widower, but it seemed that directly Roz had qualified and could earn a living, she had left home saying she must stand on her own feet and not be smothered by fatherly concern — it was true Edward did dote on her.

Now he said, 'OK then, shoot,' painting steadily on as she read out one name after another. Once or twice he interrupted — 'Oh, not him surely . . . ' or 'must we ask her?' and 'what about Pam Sutton, she's a nice kid.'

'Pam's a very nice kid, trouble is you don't keep in touch; she's gone out to Australia with her family and I can't see her flying back just to attend our wedding.'

Max came down the ladder. 'Has she? No one told me.' He picked up another brush from the table. 'I need this little 'un for the corners — carry on.' But before Roz could start again, the phone shrilled from the tiny hall. Fortunately, by pulling a few strings they had managed to get it installed; the wires had already been on the outside of the cottage and as Roz spent quite a lot of her spare time there now she had managed to persuade the local engineers to cooperate.

'Shall I go?' She put the piece of

13

paper back in the pocket of her slacks.

'No, I will. It's sure to be someone wanting to tear you away from my side and it's so seldom we can get here together, I shall tell them you're unavailable — they can't argue with that!' He grinned, wiping his fingers on a piece of rag.

Roz went to the old-fashioned sink which was still waiting to be replaced by a gleaming modern unit, and rinsed the cups in the cold spring water that came from the single brass tap.

She could hear Max's voice in the hall.

'Hullo, Governor, Peter the Painter here . . . that daughter of yours is a proper slave driver, you should have warned me, but really the place is beginning to take shape, you ought to come over and see it. If all else fails we can set up as decorators — did you want to speak to Roz?'

There was a pause as Edward obviously broke in on Max's flow of banter.

14

Then Max said in a tone of forced lightness, the banter and spontaneity gone so that involuntarily she moved towards the door to hear him say, 'Nothing serious, I hope?'

She couldn't catch her father's reply as Max put down the phone. He stood for a moment as if deep in thought, his brow furrowed, then he turned.

'The big white chief wants to see me — now — as quickly as possible, in half an hour at the most.'

He looked puzzled, and there was something else, something she couldn't quite put her finger on. It couldn't be apprehension — that was too strong a word.

'Not another promotion surely?' she said quickly, as if to relieve the sudden tension she was conscious of.

His expression changed — he grinned as he bent to kiss her. But she noticed the grin didn't reach his eyes, and his lips were icy cold.

A little shiver went down her spine.

2

They had driven out to the cottage in Roz's Mini, and Max chafed a little at having to drive more slowly than in his own Jag, which would have eaten up the miles between the cottage and the town where the Henson's Electronics factory stood, and where he had a flat. He toyed with the idea of going there first to change from his paint stained jeans and sweat shirt, but there had been something in Edward's tone which had aroused his anxiety. Roz had been right — it was as if he were about to be reprimanded. He couldn't imagine what for. His mind went round and round like a hamster on a wheel, going over the last few hours at the plant, the days before, trying to winkle out anything that could have caused trouble. Like the film from a movie camera, he went through all the different facets of their work with lasers.

There were civil applications, metal cutting, the new discs for video and stereo. It was incredible how far the work had gone in the twenty years or so since laser as a source of light had been discovered in nineteen-sixty. As he had said to Roz, you had to keep your mind alert, all the time you learned.

Recently a new development had been discovered quite by accident in their laboratory. He wondered if it might be something to do with that. Although it could be of use in a military sense, it wasn't exactly top secret, but they had been told not to talk about it. It had something to do with distances, the transference of messages by telephone or television between any two points; they had discovered a method of extending the distance which could be of vital use during a war . . .

Another thought had occurred to him as he drove up on to the motorway which led to a kind of small spaghetti junction before the town, which had spread like some cancerous growth, its tentacles stretching into the beautiful countryside. That was partly why he and Roz wanted so desperately to get away from it all for both of them loved the country.

The thought that had come to bother him now was the big order in Scandinavia which he had managed to pull off in the face of both German and Japanese competition only last month. Was it possible they had changed their minds and cancelled? He had been so pleased, particularly with the wedding drawing near, that he had justified himself to Edward.

Coming from a poor family and having had to pull himself up by his bootstraps, working part time at a job to get himself through university, he was jealous always of his ability, vulnerable, even sometimes lacking in self-confidence. The obtaining of this big contract which ensured work for the plant for months to come, had been an enormous ego boost, a real feather in his cap.

Edward had taken them out to dinner to celebrate.

Deciding it was best not to waste time changing, he drove through the gates of the plant, giving a mock salute to the man in his little gatehouse. Already he was trusted virtually as one of the family, most of the staff and workers knew and liked Max — he had no side.

As he reached Edward's outer office he was surprised to see Lee Firth, his secretary, at her desk.

'Hullo, what's this? Working on Saturday . . . shall have to tell the Union about this,' he grinned at her, trying to show a lightness of heart he didn't somehow feel.

She looked up, but there wasn't the usual wide mouthed smile he got from her and the other girls; she looked almost wary.

'What's all the flap about? I thought I'd better not even stop to change.' He looked down at his paint stained jeans and hands. 'Think it'll matter?'

A ghost of a smile touched the edges of her mouth, but she didn't look straight at him still, shrugging her shoulders.

'I wouldn't really know — about changing, I mean — and I've no idea why Mr Henson wants to see you; he just told me it was urgent and to try the cottage.' She paused a moment, then she did look at him, and now there seemed to be more pity than anything else in her eyes.

'There are two men in there with him. He didn't say who they are, just told me they were coming, that they didn't need to identify themselves and to let them in. I asked him if he wanted tea or coffee, or anything, but he said no. I think they must have rung him from the airport because they came in a taxi, and he rang me at home and then picked me up, said there might be notes he wanted taken, which seemed odd. He's got the audio machine he uses at weekends, but there were a lot of files to dig out . . . '

She suddenly stood up as if she felt she had said too much, been too friendly.

'I think you'd better go straight in, it seemed urgent.'

Max knocked and walked in without waiting for Edward to say come in. It was the usual procedure.

Two men sat either side of the desk, facing Max. As the door opened they got to their feet. For a moment, as if a film had stopped, no one moved or spoke, then Edward said, 'This is Max Pierce, gentlemen.' He turned to Max. 'These men are from Special Branch, Max. It seems they want to talk to you.'

For no reason he could think of, for certainly his conscience held no guilt — he was on his guard. He couldn't imagine in his wildest dreams what they could want, in fact the very words Special Branch simply conjured up a picture of some wildly improbable television play. He felt sure he must be dreaming; in a moment he would wake and realise none of it was really happening.

Was this what people meant when they said they had to pinch themselves to make sure they were awake?

The men still stood where they were. Max, too, was motionless. Edward had sat down again. Max smiled, although his lips felt tight over his teeth, a travesty of a grin.

'Well, well, gentlemen, whatever I can do to help — but I'm afraid you have me completely foxed. I'm not even sure what Special Branch do, what their function is — apart from what we see on the telly.'

The men gave no indication that they had even heard what he said.

Edward got up again.

'I think it would probably be best if I left you alone . . . '

For a moment Max thought perhaps the men had come to discuss security about the new use of the laser. But he dismissed the idea at once. Why with him? Surely that was Edward's province.

Suddenly what Edward had just said, sunk in and he said quickly, 'Good heavens, no, I've absolutely nothing to hide. I'd much rather you stayed.'

The elder of the two men introduced himself.

'I'm Detective Sergeant Perry and this is Detective Constable Moore.' He paused a moment, cleared his throat uncomfortably. 'There are just one or two things we want to clear up, Mr Pierce. Please sit down.' He glanced now at Edward, not meeting Max's eyes. Edward had sunk into his chair again. He waved his hand a trifle impatiently.

'Of course, sit down, all of you.'

The sergeant had a file in his hand to which he now referred.

'You did a spell of work for the firm in Germany, I believe Mr Pierce?'

Of course Max remembered, it had been five . . . no six . . . years ago. He hadn't been with the firm long when

Edward had sent him to Berlin. He'd been tickled to death being entrusted with the mission, which was important.

'Yes, that's quite right, but I — '

The sergeant went on. 'You were there for a fortnight in the June of nineteen seventy-five, you stayed at the Bremen in West Berlin, it had no restaurant, and you used to go out for your dinner . . . In East Berlin you stayed at a small hotel in the Marx Engels Place, overlooking a park and the River Spree.'

God, I wonder if they know the colour of the pyjamas I was wearing — or not wearing, Max thought. A cold shiver ran down his spine. It couldn't be true, they knew every movement it seemed, they were frighteningly accurate. The details of times, places . . . the sergeant's voice went droning on.

Fear, anxiety now, were making Max edgy.

At last he burst out, 'What the hell is all this about? You've made your point, Big Brother was watching me. Am I suspected of being some kind of spy, mole or whatever you call them? I really very much resent this intrusion into my privacy.'

With deliberate concentration, the sergeant went on, 'Did you know a Sybille Klein, Mr Pierce?'

It was the last thing he had dreamed of being asked. But as they had been going through the routine of his programme in Berlin, he had remembered . . . thought about her, of course, but not that the sergeant's questions were leading to her . . .

He inclined his head.

'Yes, I knew Fraulein Klein, but I don't see . . . '

'How well?'

The sergeant's tone had lost its rather honeyed sweetness now; it was as if he had drawn a steel blade from the velvet cover in which he had had it concealed. The cards now were down on the table.

For a moment Max didn't answer. Anyhow how did you answer a question like that to total strangers?

'How well?' the sergeant repeated, the words coming out almost like rifle shots.

Slowly Max turned and looked at him now.

'Well, enough to intend marrying her — if it's any of your business . . . '

3

Edward got quickly to his feet as if he, too, could not stand the drift of the questions, the probing — or indeed, the sergeant's attitude.

'Look, all this is on file, it's obvious you know about the entire affair so what is the point of going on asking these questions? Apart from anything else I can't see their relevance and they must be very painful for Max — Mr Pierce — I can't imagine he was deeply involved with this girl.'

But now Max looked at Edward, gently shaking his head.

'That isn't quite correct; it wasn't like that. I was in love with Sybille Klein.'

Once more Edward sank back into his chair. He was basically a simple man emotionally and all this was getting beyond him; he had an air now of deflation, resignation almost.

'It's quite straightforward, I assure you. The only thing I didn't tell you really was the whole story when I got back from Berlin.' Max took out a cigarette and lighted it, then realising what he'd done he raised his brows at Edward.

'I'm sorry, do you mind?'

Edward shook his head.

'I didn't tell you all of it,' Max went on, 'because at the time I couldn't bear to speak of it. Sybille Klein lived behind the Iron Curtain with her mother. That is where we met. They were dining at the restaurant not far from the hotel where I stayed in Marx Engels Place — as the sergeant already so accurately told us.' There was an edge of sarcasm to his voice. He'd been rattled, there was no doubt about it. It was quite terrifying to find out all one's movements had been recorded, watched, noted. You heard of these things but like fatal accident and illness, you just couldn't imagine they could happen to you.

He continued a little more slowly, memory was painful. 'There had been some confusion over the tables, the head waiter had booked us both at the same one, so we shared. That is the first time we met. Her mother was not strong, and Sybille had to do a job to help out, served in some kind of shop in the district nearby, otherwise they couldn't have afforded the treatment her mother needed.'

His mind ran on ahead and he wondered now if it was also on the file that he and Sybille had become lovers. He hated the idea of the exposure, it was like being stripped naked before a crowd. Although it was something from the past it had been precious, indestructible, no one could take it from him. His first true, rapturous love, an April love. However much one loved again, it could never be quite the same. He remembered the words of a song — Nevermore it was called — nevermore will things be quite the same. It was true.

The sergeant's voice cut harshly into his reverie.

'Please go on, Mr Pierce.'

Max hadn't realised he'd stopped speaking. He ground out the half smoked cigarette. It was years since he had taken out this little piece of his past and examined it. It hurt — desperately.

'I made several trips to Germany over a period of months — as of course you will know,' he said with irony. 'Eventually I arranged to bring Sybille to the Western Sector. I was going to fly her from there back to England. We should have been married.' It was like opening up an old, half forgotten wound.

The sergeant was tapping his teeth with his pencil. It was the only sound in the waiting silence, apart from a fly which had got caught in a spider's web and was buzzing in the window — and now he could hear his own heartbeat. He felt just like that fly, caught in a web he hadn't even known existed.

Sybille — her image rose before his inner eye. She had been strikingly beautiful, more Slav than German with high cheek bones, dark hair, black eyes like a gipsy — and a wonderful figure.

'I arranged to have her smuggled out. It was going to be a very professional job. There are dozens of them over there — these dealers in human lives and misery — or there were, I don't know what happens now. They'd do it if you had enough cash. Somehow I scraped it together.' He paused again, remembering . . .

'I waited at the checkpoint, one of the smaller ones.' He hesitated for a moment, certain the sergeant must be able to fill in this piece of information.

He was not disappointed. The man shuffled the papers in the file, cleared his throat.

'The Chaussestrasser . . . ' For a moment the word hung in the quiet of the room — he had waited in the thin grey drizzle which always seemed to fall near the wall, whatever the weather in other parts of Berlin. The minutes had passed, turned into hours. He knew something must have gone wrong, badly wrong.

Then suddenly he had heard the sound of an engine, drawing nearer hope sprang again. But only a motor bike loomed out of the mist and darkness. He was about to turn away again but the rider came over and held out a piece of paper, then thrust it at him. 'Herr Pierce?'

Max nodded. Before he could speak the man had gone.

Slowly he unfolded the paper . . .

There had been an accident. The lorry had hit a mine in a freshly laid field the driver had not known about. Everyone in the vehicle, including Fraulein Sybille Klein, had been killed instantly.

As he finished speaking there was silence again.

Edward got up, almost tipping over his chair in his haste.

'Max, my dear boy, I am so sorry, I had no idea . . . '

Max shrugged. 'Of course not. It was

not something I felt I could discuss then, and as time passed there seemed no point. Now — well it is just something that happened in the past. It is sad, tragic, but I suppose it is happening every day.'

As he spoke, the sergeant got up and came over to him, holding out a photograph.

'Is this the woman?'

Max took the photo from him. It was out of focus, blurred, but even so it was obvious it could not be Sybille.

He shook his head.

'No, this time I'm afraid you're wrong, Sergeant. Sybille was in her early twenties, she looked even younger. That certainly is not her, that is some middle-aged woman.'

The policeman said drily, 'Yes, but the time you are talking about was six years ago, sir.'

Max felt he had reached breaking point with the sergeant. He didn't like his attitude at all, neither did he like the fact that he made him feel guilty of something, something of which he had no idea, as if he were about to be accused of some crime and would have no defence . . .

'Look here,' he got to his feet, almost throwing the photo back at the sergeant, 'she died six years ago, I don't know why you have to bring this up now, why the past has to be dug out. It's painful to say the least, and quite unnecessary. Who the lady is in your photo I haven't the slightest idea, or who has put you up to all this, but one thing I can tell you — that is not Sybille Klein.'

It was then that life seemed to take on a kind of nightmare quality.

'I am afraid you were misinformed, sir,' the sergeant said with great deliberation. 'Sybille Klein was not killed. There is a lady waiting at Heathrow now, she is being held temporarily by Immigration as her papers are not quite in order, something to do with a visa, but she gave us your name and that of this firm. She was absolutely definite about both.

'She also said she was engaged to be married to you and is prepared to swear an affidavit that her name is Sybille Klein . . . '

4

For a few seconds Max didn't move. He was so stunned by the events of the last few moments he felt as though he had been physically assaulted. It was the kind of situation from which you woke thankfully — a nightmare.

If it were really true that Sybille Klein herself was waiting at the airport, how could it be that she was alive? He had been assured of the fact that she was dead by that messenger on the motor bike, that of course had not been sufficient to satisfy him and he had made all the enquiries he could, discreetly. He had been as certain as it was possible that she was dead, the lorry had hit a mine and everyone inside had been killed; there had even been quite a long piece about it in the West Berlin papers. Short of going back into the eastern zone and making more detailed enquiries, which would undoubtedly have led to his being arrested and interrogated, there had been nothing more he could do but accept the terrible information as the truth.

He had thought of trying to contact Frau Klein, Sybille's mother, but that might jeopardise her safety more than what already occurred had done. There would be sure to be some kind of punishment meted out to any relative of an escapee — he had heard of these things many times before.

And now he thought of Roz, suddenly realising he hadn't thought of her at all during the sergeant's revelations. He had gone back entirely to the past, relived that time and all else had been erased from his mind.

Now he thought only of her, his love for her, their future, which up to an hour ago had looked so bright. This would change everything, would have to, if it was true ... If this be true — the words kept going round and round in his mind. He told himself there must be some trick somewhere — although all the time he was conscious this was only his built in self-preservation, the preservation of his own happiness that was trying to protect him from the truch. And surely, remembering what they had been to each other, he and Sybille, should he not be feeling happiness, joy even that she was alive and he was about to see her again? Pleased that she was alive of course, he wouldn't be human if that were not so, however it might affect his relationship with Roz; but that he was about to see her again, of that he was not so sure.

'I should be glad if you could arrange to come back to Heathrow with me Mr Pierce. It would help to straighten things out at that end.'

The sergeant's voice brought him back to the immediate present. He got to his feet. His knees felt weak as though he had been ill in bed for weeks. He put out his hand and supported himself on the edge of Edward's desk. The smooth wood felt cool to his touch, automatically he ran his finger along the leather edge where it met the wood, a kind of reassurance that he was awake.

'I . . . ' his mouth was dry, he found it difficult to speak, to think even of the words he needed to utter.

Edward seemed aware of his dilemma. He said quickly, 'Naturally Mr Pierce will want a little time to . . . er . . . arrange his affairs this end, Sergeant. Is there any immediate rush?'

His eyes were on Max. He knew what he was thinking. That he had to talk to Roz before he could go with the police to the airport. He had somehow to explain to her what he was about to do, who was waiting for him — and what their relationship had been — what the woman who waited might be expecting it still to be.

Edward was not a man of great imagination; his brain was shrewd, direct, fantasy he left to others, but he had a deep affection for this young man and a great love for his daughter. He realised what Max must be suffering.

The sergeant glanced at his watch.

'I had said we'd be back in London tonight — Mr Pierce with me, but I appreciate he may need a little time to change and so on.' He glanced at Max's painted stained jeans and shirt. 'Perhaps you would prefer to catch a later flight then, sir?'

'I'd rather drive down,' Max said quickly. He'd have time to think, to adjust, driving down the motorway — an aeroplane would be too quick, too distracting, anyway he hated flying.

'I shall have to get in touch with my headquarters,' the sergeant said. 'It is a question really of keeping Fraulein Klein waiting — it will mean she will have to be found accommodation — that kind of thing.'

Max was struggling to find his balance as it were, trying to get his movements over the next few hours sorted into some kind of sequence — logical sequence. He had never felt less logical, his mind seemed to be clouded as if he were battling through a tangible fog that filled his mind, clogged his mental faculties.

'I'll drive down overnight, Sergeant, if that's agreeable.'

The sergeant nodded, got out his notebook and wrote something in it, tearing out the sheet and handing it to Max.

'Very well, sir. I'd be glad if you'd report at that office directly you reach Heathrow. Meanwhile I will see arrangements are made for the lady to stay at the Skyways hotel.' He paused a moment, tapping his teeth with his pencil, which for some reason annoyed Max.

'That point is, sir — it's rather a delicate one — I gather the lady hasn't very much money with her — I don't know . . . ' his voice faded out.

Edward quickly came to the rescue,

grasping the point which for the moment seemed to have completely eluded Max.

'Don't worry about that; I shall of course be responsible for any expense the lady may incur.'

The sergeant inclined his head. 'Thank you, sir. Perhaps you would be good enough just to let me have confirmation of that in some form.' He had the grace to look a little sheepish as he made the request and added, 'Just for the records, you know.'

Edward nodded. 'I'll get my secretary to deal with it.'

Max opened his mouth to try and protest, but no words came out. However, he had by now managed to pull himself into some kind of shape, although his mind still felt in a fog, fuzzy round the edges . . .

'Shall I send a works car out to the cottage to pick up Roz?' Edward had his hand on the phone; he had seen the little Mini in the car park and guessed she had no transport.

'No, not that, please, not whatever ... ' Max stumbled over the words. He knew he had to go and tell her now, without any delay, without the shock of a firm's car coming for her.

'I'll go myself, if you like,' Edward said gently.

But Max shook his head vehemently, reaching into the pocket of his jeans for his car keys, an automatic action.

The drive back to Badger's Holt was such a contrast to his drive into town that if his mind had not been in the state it was, had he been able to look at the whole situation in a detached manner, it would have been unbelievable that in so short a time he could have swung from the peak of joy to deep despair — and yet why did he feel despair? Surely a wraith from the past could not destroy the present? And yet it seemed Sybille was more than a wraith; she had been his first love, the object of that first fine careless rapture that only comes once in a lifetime. He remembered hearing the lesson read once in church with the words 'Where your treasure is, there will your heart be also . . . ' Once that had been true of Sybille.

His driving, too, was in contrast to the other trip — now he drove slowly, wishing the journey could go on forever with no conclusion, his mind running on ahead of his physical presence. He still had no idea what he would say to Roz, and even less how she would take it.

How true it was that we never really know another human being, however long we may live with and love them — Roz was sincere, deeply compassionate, but still a woman in love with a man — her man. How primitive this feeling of possessiveness in her would be he could not guess. He tried to put himself in her position but it wasn't easy. Men and women had widely differing values . . .

★　★　★

The twilight of the spring evening was turning to dusk, the shadows of the trees growing long on the lawn.

Roz kept glancing now at her watch, worrying that Max might have had an accident, wondering what on earth could have kept him all this time. There was something quite eerie about the little cottage now that she had never noticed before, although she'd been alone there often enough, either working in the garden or measuring up for curtains, now somehow it seemed as though it were waiting, watching, as she was, for Max.

She moved restlessly from room to room. She had thought of ringing the factory, but it was something she tried to avoid. It seemed like checking up on him — that was the last thing she would wish to do; perfect trust with one another was, to her, a part of loving.

She cleaned her brushes and once more went through into the downstairs room which they had had made out of two small rooms by knocking down the wall between them — she liked to call it the parlour. It was beautifully proportioned now with a big open fireplace at one end which Max had built from local stone.

She had planned where the furniture would go to the best advantage. Some of it was to be new, some she had had in her flat, taken already from her childhood home for Edward was always complaining the house was too big for one person, and urging her to return, but she was firm. She had established her independence and had no intention, much as she loved her father, of relinquishing it now.

'You see me two or three times a week anyhow,' she had laughed at him, putting her arm round him as he complained once more, 'and we get on much better when we're not under each other's feet.'

'You young people . . . ' he had muttered and gone off in a huff to play his Sunday round of golf.

Now she went up to the tiny

bathroom, tiled in warm terra cotta with the pale primrose fittings. The plumber had finished fixing the shower, although as yet no curtains surrounded it. She turned on the tap and stood back, wondering if he had managed to overcome the problem of the gravity feed. Apparently not for no water emerged. She bent forwards and looked up at the spray. At that moment a deluge of icy spring water cascaded from it, soaking her head and neck before she could draw back, running in rivulets down her sweater.

'Blast that Plod and all his works!' she exploded, looking round for something to mop herself with. All she could see was a dust sheet she had brought from home, it looked moderately clean, although it had one or two paint splashes on it, but it would have to do. She tore a strip from it wishing she had done as she wanted and had her hair shortened now as it hung round in a streaming mane, but suddenly she saw the funny side of it and started to laugh. It was just at that moment she heard the Mini draw up in the lane. Tying the piece of linen round her head turban wise, she flew down the stairs to meet Max. She reached the bottom three steps and took them in a flying leap as he came through the front door, flinging herself into his arms, the laughter bubbling up inside her.

'Max, what do you think, darling? I went up to try out the shower that dear friend Plod had fixed, and it drenched me — honestly it was just like an old Laurel and Hardy film.' She pulled the cloth from her head and the corn-gold hair tumbled round her shoulders, the damp making it curl in tight little tendrils. She looked like a small girl.

For just a moment Max held her close so that he could feel the beating of her heart against his chest, like a small bird fluttering. She was incredibly dear, never more than at this moment.

She lifted her face for the expected kiss, but almost brusquely now he pushed her away and turned to go into the kitchen. He remembered he'd left his jacket in there with his own car keys and the key to the flat.

Stunned for a moment at this change of mood, wondering what on earth could have happened, she followed him rather like a scolded child, her hands behind her back.

'Max — is something wrong? What on earth has happened? Don't tell me Pa's gone off the deep end about something?'

For a moment he didn't answer, lighting a cigarette, the flame from the match flaring up so that the beloved contours of his face were thrown into sharp relief. She felt a momentary surge of desire, a longing to cradle his head to her breast, to feel his arms about her, as if some terrible danger threatened and she needed the comfort of his nearness.

Then, slowly drawing the smoke into his lungs, feeling a momentary soothing of his raw nerves, he said, 'We have to talk, Roz. Something's happened, but I haven't much time.'

'Well, I can see that — that something's happened, I mean,' she said with a touch of asperity. Now she could see his face — because she loved him dearly and was close to him — she knew indeed that something traumatic had occurred, he seemed like a different man from the carefree, almost boyish person who had driven off a while ago as though some spell had been cast over him.

He flopped down in the old rocker that the last occupant of the cottage had left behind, automatically rocking backwards and forwards as if he was getting some kind of panacea from the movement. The rockers made a soft hissing sound on the old rug on the stone floor.

She crouched down on her haunches opposite him, still rubbing at her hair. He looked at her now, but he didn't see her, she could tell that, it was as if he looked straight through her at some ghost, some kind of apparition on the other side. He hadn't even noticed her hair was wet or heard what she said, she realised that. He was in some kind of mild shock . . . she got up and poured two mugs of coffee from the glass jug which still stood on the gas ring.

'Here, love, drink this. I'm sorry I haven't got some rum or brandy to lace it. You look as if you've seen a ghost. Nothing's happened to Pa, has it?'

Slowly he moved his head. She wasn't sure if he nodded it or shook it.

'No, nothing's happened to Edward, but you are right, I have seen a ghost — or at least heard about one I am about to see . . . '

5

Automatically he took the mug from her and started to sip the warm liquid. He did look years older, haggard as if from lack of sleep. She had seen people like it in a state of shock brought into the hospital after a pile up on the motorway, as though they had seen sights they could not believe, that their conscious minds would not accept.

Gently she covered his hand with hers.

'Tell me, Max, tell me. Nothing's so bad that I can't be of some kind of help.'

He raised his stricken eyes to her.

'I don't think you can, Roz, I don't think anyone can. It's a situation I have to face alone . . . in the ultimate we are alone . . . that's true.'

'Has someone died then?'

'No, as a matter of fact if it wasn't

such a tragic situation, that remark would be funny — it isn't that someone's died, someone's come back from the dead, just the opposite really.'

She got up. 'I don't understand.'

'Poor love, of course you don't. I'll try to explain, but quite honestly I still feel as though I've been poleaxed.'

He started to tell her about the two men from Special Branch. Then he broke off as if he'd started to tell the story from the wrong end.

'You remember I told you about a girl — a girl I was engaged to, Sybille Klein, the one I met in Germany?'

She balanced on the edge of the table, swinging her legs, still rubbing at her hair. She still couldn't understand why Max was so upset, particularly now it seemed to be something to do with this girl. He'd never talked much about her. She knew of course there had been someone before her, expected it. They had discussed the past as lovers do, but he'd never been exactly specific, in fact he'd often shut up like a clam when she had probed gently about this girl. She knew she'd died, he'd told her that much, but she had always felt his affair — if indeed it had been as much as that, had not been as serious and meaningful as they felt about each other.

She had had boy friends before — she had told him all he wanted to know about them, but with her there had never been anyone who mattered as much as Max, and she thought he had felt the same — but now she wasn't sure. She had the idea perhaps he found it too painful to discuss, but not that it had gone all that deep.

It was understandable of course that he should not have forgotten.

Max said slowly, 'I suppose it all started because I had a terrific admiration for this girl, Sybille.' As he spoke her name it made her seem a little more real, tangible. He had no alternative now but to tell Roz everything, he knew that. He wished, too, he had done this before reaching such an impasse as he found himself in now. He had never forgotten, it remained always in a corner of his mind, but gradually he had accepted what had happened. Life had to go on, an acceptance of the inevitable which couldn't be altered.

In a way it could be looked upon as if she had chosen someone else, although one could hardly suggest she would choose death for a companion at her age. Yes, it was almost as if she had married another man, only more final, so it had had to become part of the past. Had she married someone else, then doubtless when the pain had died, they might have been able to be friends; that happened all the time.

'Go on,' Roz said softly again, realising now he had been swept back into the past, that the present, the little cottage, herself, really meant nothing at this moment.

'She was so obviously a girl of good education, breeding; a gentle girl with no malice, no bitterness, although she was forced to earn her living.'

'This was in East Germany?'

'Yes. The Germans — or the Russians, I'm not sure which, had taken everything from them. Her father had died and she and her mother were harried from pillar to post. As a result of the food shortage, her mother had become ill, I don't know what it was exactly, but she needed special treatment, drugs, good food, all of which were only obtainable on the black market long after the war had finished. Then came the biggest blow of all in August 'sixty-one, when Eastern Berlin was sealed off from the West and Sybille and her mother found themselves in the Russian sector. She was just eight years old.' He paused, then he said, as if he were talking to himself, 'We can't really appreciate what it must be like to be invaded, to lose everything, suddenly to have nothing but what the state will allow you, and an alien state at that. She was only seventeen when I knew her — she'd be twenty-three now,' he paused again, 'Is twenty-three, I should say.'

'Is?' Roz stopped rubbing her hair which she'd been doing automatically while Max was talking.

He got up and went over to the little window, unable to sit any longer, to feel her eyes on him as he spoke.

'Yes. Is. She's here in England, at Heathrow. Two men from Special Branch came. That was what all the flap was about . . . they'd come to find me, to tell me. She had given them my name, the firm's address. And she's waiting at Heathrow for me now.'

He looked out at the darkening garden, surprised somehow that it all looked still the same. Then he swung round. For a moment Roz put out both her hands as if to ward off something, she didn't know what, certainly not Max himself. Perhaps this ghost from the past which now must come between them, however much both of them might deny it.

'We were lovers. I can't describe my

feelings now, but at the time it was an overwhelming feeling. I suppose in a way I'd never had anything, anyone who really belonged to me. I'd been a foster child for years, never remembered my father and mother who were both killed when I was a baby, so I've never had any family — no one to call my own.'

She moved forward now automatically, involuntarily, her hands still outstretched.

'But I . . . ' She stopped, realising Max was hardly conscious of her presence; he was simply reliving that love affair which had meant so much.

'She was naïve in many ways, and yet loving, responsive and warm, a perfect lover and companion . . . oh yes, we were lovers. At times I felt guilty, almost a seducer, she seemed such a child, but my love was sincere enough, honest — and I made plans to have her smuggled out. It seemed so logical at the time, I loved her so much. There were many people then who could arrange this, probably still are, for enough money. Swiss francs they wanted, or American dollars. Somehow I managed to get the sum they asked, it took all I had. But my love was worth it.'

'And so what happened?' Roz could hear her own heart beating as she waited for him to go on.

He lighted another cigarette from the stub of the old one, crushing it out beneath his foot.

'It was a Sunday — Bloody Sunday — I always loathed Sundays in Berlin, that part of the city. It was like a ghost town. But it seems the organisers chose this day because the checkpoints were not so fully manned or something. I didn't go into the mechanics of the whole thing, the less I knew about it the better.' He hesitated as though the words he had to speak were almost too painful to express.

'And so I waited, and waited, and still waited. I had almost decided to give up, it was pitch dark, everyone was looking at me with suspicion — those that were still about — it was bitterly cold and raining. I don't think I've ever felt so miserable, so frightened or so alone, but it was all going to be worth it when I saw that beloved face.'

Roz put out her hand. 'Poor love, so then what?'

'Suddenly I heard the sound of an engine — oh it must have been nearly two hours I'd been waiting. I'd hidden in one of the doorways; actually this was one of the lesser known checkpoints, that's why they'd chosen it. They had special forged papers, all that kind of thing; they knew the ropes, been doing it for years. Anyway I heard this engine, but I knew it wasn't a lorry, something much smaller. It turned out to be a motor bike. The chap looked like some kind of military despatch rider. I didn't particularly want him to see me, but I couldn't avoid it. He rode straight up to me as if he was certain who it was waiting, and thrust a piece of paper into my hand. I nearly let it drop I was so surprised, as he said roughly — 'Herr Pierce?' I nodded and he said, 'They told me to give you this. She won't be coming, the Fraulein.'

Before I could gather my wits together, ask him anything, he'd gone and I was left with this piece of paper in my hand. I got out my cigarette lighter to read it. It was written in German. My German isn't all that good, but I could just make out the words and her name — Fraulein Sybille Klein, the fact that she, with all the others in the lorry, had been killed, blown up on a mine. I can't describe to you how I felt, it was as if the world had ended. I went back to my hotel and got blind drunk, there just wasn't anything else to do.

'At first I had ideas of trying to make some enquiries, to check up and make sure it was true, but over in East Berlin it's . . . well it's difficult to describe, but you just can't get any sense out of anyone, like the wall itself, you're up against a dead end all the time. And of course if you try probing too deeply, asking too many questions, you're in real trouble.'

For a moment there was silence, then Roz said, 'So you came back to England, but why didn't you tell anyone? Pa, for instance.'

'I don't know really, I felt I couldn't talk about it to anyone, and there was something else, too.' He paused. 'You see I was haunted by the feeling that if I hadn't tried to get her out, persuaded her, she wouldn't have been killed, I had a terrible feeling of guilt.'

She put her arm along his shoulders, but he was quiescent as if he didn't feel her touch.

'And now they tell you it isn't true, that she wasn't killed at all?'

'That's what they say. They showed me a photograph of some middle-aged woman, I'm sure it isn't Sybille — and yet there was something about the eyes, she had beautiful eyes, so expressive. But of course this isn't coloured, this photo, it could be anyone. All I can do is believe them when they say she is at

Heathrow asking for me. But I simply can't see the reason behind it, or how she managed to escape being killed when everyone else was — neither can I even guess who it was came to tell me it was so — ' He broke off abruptly as if a sudden thought had struck him, then shook his head saying softly, 'No, that couldn't be . . . so,' he went on, 'I have no alternative but to go and see if this woman is who she says she is, I suppose, although what I'm meant to do then I don't know, I'm not sure . . . Oh God, I'm not sure of anything.' He dropped his head wearily on his hands. He couldn't really explain why this had affected him as it had, he supposed it was the shock, the terrible shock of someone seeming literally to come back from the dead, the doubt whether it was true or not, and the memories . . .

Roz stood looking down at him, her heart too full to speak. This was the man she loved — loved as well as was in love with, for those were two very different things, that she knew. She realised from the way he had spoken of her that this girl had been something special, very special — a true first love — as he was now for her for she had only fancied herself in love before, there had never been anyone like Max, this she knew with certainty. Now she knew, too, or guessed that perhaps there was no one for this German girl either but Max, the fact that six years had passed could mean nothing, might mean nothing if Max had been her first love, too, and she were as innocent and naïve as he had said.

Obviously if there had been some accident she would have been in hospital, suffered from amnesia perhaps, and the lapse of time might be explained thus — now she wanted Max, to revive the past as it had been.

Being a woman herself Roz could appreciate this.

As for Max, it was difficult to assess the situation from a man's point of view, but however he felt, there was going to be need for readjustment.

'I can't understand why, if she wasn't killed, she has been so long getting in touch,' he muttered.

'Maybe she's been in hospital. In any case, as you know yourself, have already said, living behind the Iron Curtain is scarcely the same as being in Britain. Perhaps it has taken her all this time to get permission, visas and so on to come to England, particularly if they know she had been planning to defect.'

'Yes, I suppose that could be it.'

'Anyway,' she went on slowly, 'we must be practical, for the moment at least we must postpone our wedding plans — we owe her that until we have found our more details, tried to find out what she wants — expects.'

Max looked at her, so lovely, so desirable. Slowly he was trying to analyse his own feelings, to get things in their true perspective. Some of his memories of Sybille were painful, some were happy, but he had had to come to terms with losing her, to acknowledge it had been over and was part of the past, and yet, because of that past, he could not refuse to see her, to talk to her, to acknowledge her — if it were truly her.

It felt as if his world had fallen apart at the seams, and he supposed in some ways, Roz's as well, although in the ultimate surely it could not part them.

He got up and poured out the rest of the coffee. It was cold and tasteless, bitter on his tongue but it fitted in with his mood.

'I shall have to go home and change and leave for Heathrow at once to meet . . . ' He found it difficult to say her name to this woman he loved, cherished and intended to marry.

She took his hand and held it to her cheek, her heart-shaped, delicate face serious and intent.

'I'll come with you, darling. She may need someone, something to trust in, we all do, Max,' she said softly.

He rested his chin on the damp,

corn-gold hair which smelled of summer flowers.

'No, my love, this is something I have to face alone, quite alone,' he said slowly.

6

Back at Roz's flat they tried to swallow food. She had insisted that after he had showered, changed and picked up his own car he must have something before he left.

'God knows when you'll get anything otherwise. I know you, you just won't stop once you leave here, and an hour now isn't going to make all that much difference after six years.' She had difficulty in keeping just a hint of bitterness out of the last few words.

It was strange . . . not strange that she had a feeling of apprehension at this girl — woman, she supposed she was now — coming back into Max's life, but strange how for the first time since they had known each other, been in love, it was as if a door had shut between them. For the first time they found it difficult to talk, there would be a silence; then they would both start to speak — not about what was foremost in their minds, but about something trivial. 'Worcester sauce or mustard on your steak?' — 'Would you like cheese or fruit? Shall I make the coffee now?'

Strangers because this woman, this shadow from the past had suddenly come between them; intangible she might be at the moment but even that had already changed things between them.

It was long after midnight when at last she watched the twin ruby lights of the Jag disappear round the corner of the quiet road where she had her flat. She stood on the steps for a moment, her finger to her lips where he had kissed her. His mouth had felt cold, his lips dry, and she knew her own were unresponsive.

They had been lovers, this woman and Max. She was not so stupid as to think he had never slept with anyone before he met her, wouldn't even have wanted it, but now that the recipient of that love, passion, was about to be thrust into her life, that was different.

All kinds of pictures, scenes, ran unbidden through her mind.

With a gesture of impatience she went back into the flat. She needed something violent to do — no, not violent, something challenging, all absorbing, but there was nothing — it was the middle of the night ... the spring sky was bright with stars, the air mild for the time of year and heavy with the perfume of wall-flowers from someone's window box. Suddenly they brought back memories, a little country church where her father had taken her when she was quite a small girl, it must have been soon after her mother died. She supposed they must have been on holiday. The spring day then had been warm and the church door open whilst the service was held; through the door had come the perfume of wallflowers. Now, for some ridiculous reason, she burst into tears, the sobs tearing at her throat and chest so that she had trouble in breathing, gasping as if she were drowning, worried for a moment she would wake the occupants of the other flats.

It was the longest night she ever remembered. She made pints of coffee, washed the supper things, wandered from room to room thinking it would never be dawn. It was her day off from the hospital for which she was thankful. She couldn't possibly have faced her friends, the people who had known her for years, who understood her every mood, and who would know at once something was wrong, badly wrong.

She gazed at her face in the mirror. Talk about Max not being able to recognise Sybille, she thought with a rueful grin at her reflection, I look like something out of a horror movie!

As when she had been a child, when things went awry in her world, her father had been the one she ran to, the rock she clung to. Now, as soon as it was light and she had showered, splashed her face with cold water and tried to hide the worst of the ravages with make-up, she went down and got out the Mini, driving slowly, not quite sure how to handle the situation, unsure what his reaction might be. He would know of course what she was going through — but it was no real surprise he hadn't been round to see her; he would know she had to be alone and that when she needed him she would make the first move.

He was having his breakfast, the Financial Times propped against the coffee pot, thick marmalade in the cut glass bowl, the silver chafing dishes on the side; all as it had been since she could remember. Meg Tangye, the housekeeper, had been with her father since Roz was a little girl, and she made sure the house ran on oiled wheels.

'She spoils you rotten,' Roz had said once. 'Does it ever occur to you that poor woman has no life of her own? She's completely dedicated to your comfort and happiness.'

He had laughed and drawn her into

the circle of his arms. 'That's what you think. Meg Tangye told me her life here was ideal, she loves cooking and housework, has a good home, she never really wanted a husband, and when she got one he was a drunken oaf who beat her. Mercifully he was killed during the war instead of being run over by a bus, which I don't doubt he richly deserved; at least it appeared as if he had a death fit for heroes.'

Now he looked up from the paper and held out his arms. 'I thought you'd come, my darling child. Pour yourself some coffee, and you'd better see what's left in those dishes on the side, you look as if you could do with a square meal.'

'That's a very tactful way of telling me I look like some disaster area. Coffee, please, but I couldn't eat just now; I shan't fade away yet.' She attempted a weak smile which died before it reached her eyes. She sank down in the chair next to him. He put out his hand and covered hers with it.

'Don't worry too much. I have a feeling all this can be resolved.'

She glanced at him quickly. 'Not with money, Pa, if that's what you think.'

He shrugged his shoulders and lit one of the small cigars he smoked instead of cigarettes, then said quickly, waving it in the air, 'Do you mind? I always forget you're trying to give it up, and it doesn't make it any easier if someone else is smoking.'

She shook her head. 'No, I'll have one now with my coffee.' She didn't tell him she'd smoked a whole packet since Max had left.

Then he said, 'I have to admit my first thought was that we could probably pay her off, that possibly this was some kind of adventuress, an imposter even who was simply after money — but now I'm not so sure.' He looked away for a moment. 'I suppose Max told you the whole story? My poor child, I'm afraid it must have been terribly painful for you.'

Roz nodded. She was cried out now.

There were no more tears and the storm she had suffered had at least acted as a relief, a bursting of the dam behind which so much emotion had built up while Max had been telling her.

'Yes, I think I can live with it, although it's not going to be easy once she arrives; it's rather different from just thinking, talking about it.'

Truth to tell Edward himself hadn't slept much. Roz was the centre of his universe, and anything that threatened her happiness was anathema. All he was interested in now was protecting her feelings.

He was still fond of Max, thought he was the right husband for Roz, and if that was what she wanted, then that was what he was going to see she had, come hell and high water. This girl had come, or was coming, into what had developed into a cosy little world the three of them shared. At first, of course, he had been reluctant to share it with a third party, but he had always known that naturally Roz would marry some day, and he had watched the various young men who had passed through his house with his daughter — metaphorically — on their arms — seen her reactions with growing confidence and admiration. He knew without doubt when she chose it would be the right choice, and Max had filled that slot to perfection. He was determined now that what he thought of as some fly-by-night girl from his past should not spoil it all. She must be kept at arm's length, shown, politely but definitely, that she was not welcome, would not fit into this world at all. And although he was not exactly cynical, he knew that every man, and woman, has their price, whatever it may be and however laudable the cause — this woman would be no different, of that he was certain.

'I suppose we should fix up some accommodation for Fraulein Klein,' he said, studying the end of his cigar. 'A hotel perhaps, or do you think she might be more comfortable in some superior type of boarding house?'

Roz got up and went over to the window, looking out across the green rolling lawns, the neatly manicured flowerbeds with their scarlet tulips and golden wallflowers — wallflowers again, she thought.

'Pa, where was that little church we went to once when I was small, it was this time of year, and they left the door open and we could smell the wall-flowers.'

He looked at her in astonishment. Really, women! You never got to know them, what a thing to think about at a time like this!

'In Devon. We'd gone down to see a distant cousin, Archie Wrangways. Fancy you remembering! You can't have been more than six or seven.'

'I'd like to be married in a little church like that.'

'You still intend to go on with the wedding than?' His voice held a note of hope.

'No, not at the moment. I am going

to start to cancel the arrangements this morning as a matter of fact. I was going to ask if I could borrow Lee to do some photocopying, make some phone calls, that kind of thing.'

'Do you think that's wise? Being quite so precipitate, rash almost. Wouldn't it be wiser to — well just to hang on and see what happens?'

'No, I know what'll happen — at least I think I do, and it's only fair to everyone that there should be no wedding in the offing, no kind of deadline to which we all have to adhere. God knows things are going to be difficult enough without that.'

He had heard that note in her voice before — when there had been something at school she didn't want to take part in, when she had told him she was moving out into her own flat and going to earn her own living.

He had learnt to acquiesce — at least for the time; he had found then sometimes things came around his way later if he didn't press them.

'Of course you can borrow Lee, as you put it.' He glanced at his watch. 'I must get on. There's quite a lot to be done and I shall miss Max for a day or two. I think we must expect him to want a little time off.'

'Yes, and I'll tell Meg to get the spare room ready, shall I?'

For a moment he thought he must have heard wrong.

'The spare room? What for, are you coming back? You'd rather have your old room surely?'

She came across to where he stood now and put her hands on his shoulders.

'No, I'm not coming back, although I shall have to find someone to share my flat now as the wedding is to be put off; that rent's too much for a poor radiologist on her own.' She managed a crooked smile now and her eyes did light up for a moment. 'No, it's for the Fraulein. I want to get to know her, to find out all about her, to see what makes her tick. We'll bring her into the house, here, into the heart of the family.'

He looked at her incredulously. 'You can't be serious?'

'Never more so.'

He knew by the set of her mouth, the tilt of her chin that it was so, and like Max, he knew what it meant when her eyes seemed dark and fathomless. It boded no good for anyone.

He grinned for a moment. 'Is this entirely altruistic, Roz?'

'No Pa.' She touched the end of his nose with her forefinger, a gesture from childhood which he knew well. 'No, it's not entirely out of the goodness of my heart, although one is bound to feel sorry for someone thrust into a family like ours unexpectedly and in a strange country. I think it is the least we can do.'

'I see.'

The two words meant more than might appear. What he saw more than anything else was the possibility that Roz had no intention of letting Max go, at least not without a fight, bloodless though it might be, and his heart felt lighter than it had done since first the two men from Special Branch had arrived at the factory.

7

Max hated Heathrow, although he knew it well enough from the various trips abroad he'd made for the firm. He'd stopped at a motel for some coffee and a smoke, not because he particularly wanted them. Usually on a journey, as Roz had said, he hated to stop, but subconsciously he was putting off this meeting which lay ahead. Anyway, he told himself, there was no point in arriving at six in the morning, two hours before his meeting with the sergeant, and obviously Sybille wouldn't be up, although she probably hadn't slept. The thought of the coming meeting must be something of an ordeal for her, too.

It was strange to arrive in the suburbs and see so little traffic; usually it had been day time as he passed through this area with vehicles buzzing in all directions. Now he reached the airport with its masses of roads, roundabouts, flyover and underpasses, quite easily with no delay. He parked the car outside the terminal building which the sergeant had described as being where the office was to which he was to report. He supposed it belonged to the airport police and that Special Branch used it when necessary.

The smell of burnt fuel hung over everything — a kind of permanent background to airports all over the world, as was the dirty, greasy deposit on everything you touched. It was like some vast city on its own and even at this time life seemed to go on much as it did during the day, cars were driving round and there was a quite frenetic coming and going.

He went into the hotel through the swing doors, he needed a wash and some coffee. The foyer was lush, characterless, could have been any-where in the world with its luxury shops, its showcases of French perfume, exquisite clothes, china, silver and huge flower arrangements which filled the air with heady perfume making his head ache. At least in there it was quiet for the place was soundproof; you were not even aware there were planes, cars and people outside.

He went into the cloakroom and taking off his coat and shirt, had a wash, then he went into the coffee bar and sat by the window which looked out across one of the landing strips. In the semi-darkness outside, the lights gleamed down from the enormous control tower and he could see planes, silent and resting now, their colours and outlines softly subdued in the early dawn light. Indians and Sikhs were arriving, he supposed to do some of the manual work in the kitchens.

In spite of the tension within him at the prospect of the coming meeting, he couldn't help feeling how insignificant his little problems were in a huge complex of this sort where hundreds of thousands of people passed through, each with a story to be told, each with problems, perhaps tragedy.

For some unaccountable reason he was sure he had been watched, followed from the moment he had arrived at the airport. He kept glancing over his shoulder; why he should feel this he didn't know, he had an absolutely clear conscience had done nothing unlawful, and yet the sight of the Special Branch men had engendered a feeling of guilt.

He drank three cups of coffee, smoked half a packet of cigarettes, and at last it was time to meet the sergeant.

As he entered the office he looked round expecting to see Sybille. He had braced himself for this moment and it was something of an anti-climax when he saw she was not there.

'Thank you for arriving early, Mr Pierce. I hope you have breakfasted.' The sergeant's face was inscrutable.

'I'm OK, thanks,' Max said shortly. All he wanted was to get the whole thing over with.

'Fraulein Klein is at the hotel. It's

only a few steps from here.'

'I've just come from there,' Max said. 'Of course, I forgot she would be there.'

'We arranged for her to stay there for the night, but I asked her to be in the lounge early.'

As they entered the half empty lounge Max experienced again the feelings he had had that dreary day long ago in Berlin when he had heard Sybille was killed — a kind of paralysis, drained of all feeling, all emotion, he even wondered if he'd be able to speak when he met her.

The sergeant led the way to a table by the window. A woman sat alone. Her head turned away. She had on a tee shirt and jeans. That couldn't be Sybille surely — always so elegant, so feminine. Then he remembered, she was still a girl, only twenty-three, tee shirts and jeans were the universal uniform of the young — and the not so young. She had cropped hair, he could see that, but what colour it was he couldn't tell for the light which came in from the window was in his eyes. He stood for a moment, hesitant. The sergeant was walking on ahead, then realising Max had stopped he turned and in an involuntary gesture, put out his hand. Max ignored it, regained some of his self-control and strode forward. The woman turned her head and looked at him. He stood quite still. It was incredible, impossible. How could that beautiful young girl have turned into this middle-aged woman who must be at least forty ... once again for a moment the thought crossed his mind that this was not Sybille, that it was some kind of hideous, cruel trick. Her cropped hair was grey, her skin lined and her cheeks sunken — but the eyes were the same, their brilliance undimmed, and the beautiful bone structure — nothing could spoil that.

The Sergeant said, 'Mr Pierce, this is Fraulein Klein.' Max took the hand she held out. It was rough and calloused, dry and cold, lying supine in his, making no effort to return the clasp he had managed to produce. She smiled, a travesty which didn't reach her eyes and inconsequentially he thought, at least she still has her own beautiful teeth.

He sat down, wondering why he felt nothing, not even pity because this was a stranger, at least so it seemed. This could not be the vibrant, laughing, glamorous girl he remembered, the girl who had lain in his arms, warm and loving with soft hands and lips.

The sergeant was speaking. 'There is no need for any more delays or formalities, Mr Pierce, all has been arranged, and it is quite in order for you to leave with Fraulein Klein at any time you wish. I am sorry you have been put to trouble and inconvenience, Fraulein. It was simply a formality, another of those unfortunate occurrences when one is travelling.'

Her eyes were downcast and Max noticed her lashes were still long and silky as they curved on the thin cheek. Perhaps with good food, rest, and some more suitable clothes . . .

She glanced up for a moment, looking at the sergeant, avoiding meeting Max's eyes. Apart from that first brief glance at their meeting, she had looked away as though she could not bear him to see her as she was now, realising the thoughts that must be going through his mind.

She got up, picking up a small case that stood on the floor, slinging a bag over her shoulder.

'Is this all your luggage?' Max took the case from her, his fingers touching hers briefly. Still he felt nothing.

She nodded. 'Yes, it is all. I have nothing . . . ' The words held so much more in their meaning that for a moment he glanced at her, but once more she looked away. The sergeant held out his hand.

'I'll say goodbye then, Mr Pierce, I hope you will have a safe journey and . . . ' Whatever it was he was going to add he evidently changed his mind.

Max held the door for her as they left the hotel.

'Would you like to wait here while I fetch the car from the park? It's only a little way.' He wasn't sure if she was ill, tired perhaps.

'I would like to walk, please.' The voice was the same, deep, husky, if he closed his eyes this could be the girl he remembered.

To his embarrassment she put her hand through his arm like a little girl. But then involuntarily he gave it a little squeeze — there was something appealing, pathetic about the gesture.

When he reached the car he opened the passenger door for her, putting her small case in the back. She clung to her shoulder bag as if her life depended on it.

'Shall I put that out of the way for you? It would be more comfortable.'

For a moment an extraordinary expression crossed her face, almost as if he had struck her — her eyes panic-stricken.

'I'm sorry, I didn't mean to upset you.' He dropped his hand.

Her taut muscles relaxed a little.

'I'm sorry. It is so stupid. I forget I am in England.' She hesitated a moment. 'You see, my passport, my visas, the things that matter are in there — I am so afraid . . . ' She stopped.

'There's nothing to be afraid of here,' he said quickly, and then thought of the men from Special Branch. Well maybe, he added to himself, that isn't strictly true.

She smiled now. 'Of course.'

He drove quickly away from the airport. The day now was clear, blue, a perfect English spring day. She seemed a little more relaxed, leaning back against the head rest, her eyes closed. He wasn't sure if she slept, he wasn't sure if she wanted to talk, he wasn't sure of anything any more. The whole thing was like a dream — not a nightmare for there was nothing to fear from this frail woman, he was sure of that, but he felt as if he moved in a dream, driving like an automaton. He had to have all his wits about him for it was rush hour, people were going to work; like ants the cars moved along the six sections of the motorway, jostling, impatient. He kept in the slow lane, but even there he had the feeling of being harassed. Once away from the suburbs it quietened a little.

'Would you like to stop for some coffee? You did have breakfast, didn't you?'

'That would be nice.' She didn't reply to his question about breakfast and he guessed like him, she hadn't been able to eat. Now she smiled and her eyes lighted up, for a moment he saw the seventeen-year-old girl as though she glanced from behind what she had become.

'I have not asked where we are going . . . '

'We have a lot to talk about, but we are going to where I live in the Midlands, a place called Dudhampton not far from Birmingham. I have a job there . . . '

He turned off the motorway and

found a small café which had just opened. The girl brought them scalding black coffee, a jug of yellow cream, warm scones and butter and jam. He watched Sybille's face as she looked at the food. For a moment an expression of almost wolfish hunger lingered on her face. He had the feeling it was only innate good manners that just prevented her from grabbing the food and cramming it into her mouth.

He passed the plate of scones. 'Please, you must be hungry and I had a good breakfast,' he lied. 'I have to watch my waistline, you know.'

She spread the butter thickly, added the jam and bit into the scone. He could sense the pleasure the food brought her.

At last she had finished and he said softly, 'Sybille.' It was the first time he had used her name. He took her hand, turning it over and examining the palm with its callouses, the half healed sores, the broken nails. Gently she withdrew it. He wondered what on earth could have caused them to be in such a state.

'Please, Max, I have to talk now, before we get to your home.'

He drew out his cigarettes and passed her one.

'Of course. We'll sit in the car, it will be more private.'

She drew the smoke deep into her lungs and then coughed. The spasm was so acute and lasted for so long, wracking her thin body, that he thought she must have some kind of fit, but eventually she stopped.

'The night, that Sunday when you waited. What did they tell you?'

'Not much. I never found out much. Oh, Sybille, I did try, really I did. I would hate you to think I had deserted you. I had no idea it was possible you were still alive. They simply told me the lorry had hit a mine, that everyone had been killed, they even specified your name as being among the dead.' He paused, the memory of that night and the emotions he had felt choking him for the moment.

She laid her hand on his.

'I can imagine. But you see I was lucky.' She caught her breath. 'Lucky — that is hardly the word perhaps, for it might have been better if I had been killed, or so I often thought, but I was thrown clear. Everyone else was killed, that was true.' She hesitated a moment, glancing away at the green fields, the trees, the spring sunshine and the wild flowers. He could see she found it hard to believe she actually was in England. 'Everyone else but me. I was badly hurt, at first they thought I would not recover; both my legs were broken, my skull fractured, I had lost much blood, oh, I was hardly alive, that is true. Of course, I remember nothing, I was unconscious, remained so for days, but it seems they had not found me for several hours. I had been thrown into a cornfield; no one had thought of looking there, until they counted the dead and found one missing . . . then they searched, worried of course that I had escaped. Then they found me.' She paused again. 'Perhaps it would have been better if they had not,' she said softly, and added so quietly that he wasn't sure if he had heard her, 'better perhaps for all of us . . . '

8

Max drove slowly. Now that Sybille had started to talk it seemed she couldn't stop, as if all the words which had accumulated inside for so long — six long years — must now burst out in a torrent. Sometimes her English was so confused he couldn't understand — sometimes she lapsed into German.

Whilst she talked she took a small mirror from her bag, ran a comb through her hair, and put on some lipstick, then she turned to him.

'You did not recognise me! It is not surprising. I am hardly the girl you once loved.'

He lifted his hand from the wheel in a gesture of protest, but she went on, 'As a punishment I was sent to a labour camp. I was in the camp for six years. To me it was two lifetimes. You have read of German labour camps — the

Russian ones make those seem like what you call the holiday camp. I was made to stay there as a punishment, to work to repay the authorities for the time I had been in hospital.'

'Then they released you?'

'My time was up. The punishment over. They had, I think, lost interest in me.'

'But I don't understand . . . '

'Please,' she turned and put a finger to his lips, 'I do not want to talk about it. Sufficient that I am here, and perhaps it is better you know nothing.' She paused a moment. 'It is strange, you see, I had no idea you thought me dead. I just thought you had possibly written, tried to get in touch, but that they had kept the information from me. This is usual. When the time came, they made no protest, no particular difficulty over my papers, visas and so on. I said I was coming to England, hoped to see old friends. There were not even hints about the true position.'

'But I can't see . . . I don't know

. . . I am so confused. Of course I imagined . . . if I had only known where you were, that you were alive, I would have done all in my power . . . but this is England . . . when you say it is better I know nothing . . . nothing about what? I don't quite understand.'

For a moment she looked away, then she said, 'Yes, in England I can see you do not understand, but it is so wonderful to see you. Even in West Berlin sometimes they do not understand, although the Russians could come across any time, any day.

'Do you know, there is a Museum, it is called the Checkpoint Charlie Museum — perhaps the most remarkable in the world, for it is a collection of the different methods used by desperate human beings, like trapped animals, to get out . . . there is the hot air balloon in which two families sailed over the wall. Such a contrast to the very low sports car which a driver drove under the barriers to the western side before the guards had a chance to realise what was happening. But so many deaths, so much bloodshed.'

'I think I do understand,' he said slowly. 'Don't forget I stood by that wall once, waiting for you. That seemed like a lifetime, ending in death.'

'I know; do not think I am ungrateful.' She sighed.

'This year the wall will be twenty years old. Only three younger than I.'

As they neared the Midlands Max knew he had to tell her about Roz . . . As if she had read his mind, she said, 'You are not married, I think?'

He let out his breath on a long sigh. He had known it had to come. But how to handle it he did not know.

'No,' he said slowly, 'I am not married. But I am sure you will understand — I thought you were dead. I made every enquiry I could, explored every possibility, even to the extent of nearly getting imprisoned myself, but everyone assured me you were dead.'

'So, there is someone else, is that what you try to say?'

'There is someone, yes. We are . . . were . . . to be married. She's quite something, a wonderful person. Under different circumstances you would perhaps have been friends.'

She smiled, but it didn't quite reach her eyes as she said, 'And being a man, under present circumstances you think we cannot?'

'It would be asking a lot of both of you. You see for her — and I suppose for me, too — it is as if you have returned from the dead — please don't misunderstand me, for it to have happened is a miracle, but . . . '

'But as you feel, although you do not say, it is difficult to adjust, for you and for this — what is her name, I do not think you said.'

'Roz — Rosalind. It's her father, Edward Henson who is my boss.'

'This I understand, this question of adjusting, but even if I do not look like the Sybille you remember, underneath, inside here,' she drew his hand to her breast so he could feel the beating of her heart, 'in there I am the same. I remember the things we did together, what we shared, that we were in love and lovers.'

'I know that.' Gently he disengaged his hand and put it back on the wheel.

'But it is difficult to accept this knowledge. I can understand that, too, but all the same it is a fact.'

Because he was driving and had his eyes on the road he could not see her expression, could not tell if she were intending to be inflexible in her attitude, or simply stating the case as she saw it.

He knew it wasn't fair, but there was only one person now he could appeal to to straighten out the mess he was in, the last person he should have gone to, but nevertheless he had to. Roz.

Roz was back in her flat. She felt composed now, in some odd way detached as though it were all happening to someone else. She had come to terms with the situation as far as she could before she actually met the whole cause of it. She guessed Max would bring Sybille to see her first, in any case when he left there had been no decision made where she was to stay, she knew he would be feeling confused and uncertain. At least it was some comfort, some satisfaction to guess he would need her.

She heard his car and ran down to the main entrance to the flats. It would be easier to meet them there than just wait — some form of attack is always better than defence she told herself.

When she first saw Sybille getting out of the Jag she thought there must be some mistake, just as Max himself had. This middle-aged woman, all skin and bone, couldn't be the girl he had described to her. Surely nothing could have changed her all that much in just six years.

Sybille turned and saw Roz at the top of the steps and straightened her back. She glanced up; the expression on her face was difficult to assess from that distance, but Roz knew it was a challenge of some kind. Here were two women fighting for their man and both of them were going to use every weapon they had, but she held out her hand; she could be wrong, it could be that even female intuitiveness let you down sometimes.

Sybille came slowly up the steps towards her, Max hovering a little uncertainly in the background. He knew Roz well enough to know her good manners would triumph over any other feelings she might have, he also knew she was a woman, that she loved him and he loved her.

She had cut sandwiches, prepared hot soup. They had a drink first after she had shown Sybille where the bathroom was and offered make-up and so on.

Max gulped his whisky and Roz refilled his glass.

'Was it too awful?'

He shook his head slowly. 'I don't know, yes, I suppose it was in a way. When I first saw her I simply couldn't believe it, but she's been a prisoner in a labour camp, poor kid . . . '

'You are sure it is Sybille Klein?' Roz asked quickly.

'Yes, certain. They couldn't change those eyes or that voice — and the mannerisms, little things one remembers about someone . . . ' He paused. Roz turned away quickly and poured herself another drink. Little things — about someone you love, that's what he was going to say, she thought. Little intimate things one remembers about a love, a first love.

He went on telling Roz some of what Sybille had told him. They were still talking of it when Sybille returned, her face scrubbed like a small child's, innocent of make-up, but Roz could see the bone structure, the underlying beauty which as Max, too, had thought, with good food and rest could be restored to some extent, although there was a kind of haunted look about her eyes.

The drink helped to make the

atmosphere a little easier. To start with Sybille talked of the Germany she had remembered as a child, then of the labour camp.

As she talked Roz felt herself warming to her. Now and then there were flashes of humour and wit which once must have been part of her personality, and, too, an innate gentleness when she spoke of children, of animals, or people and the countryside where she had been brought up. At times, even now, her face became quite beautiful with animation, but for some reason Roz had an increasing feeling that she wasn't telling the whole truth about her release from the camp.

Her first natural antagonism had worn thin now; she liked this woman and she was glad she had suggested she stay with Edward — although at the time she had to admit her aims had not been all for Sybille's benefit. Now she thought, it will give me a chance to find out what she really is after. Somehow

— and the thought was comforting — she was pretty sure it wasn't Max himself . . .

'I hope you will be comfortable at Old House,' she said at last. 'My father is out most of the time, and the housekeeper is a dear person. She'll make you very welcome, and it is a huge place; it's just a waste to go to a hotel when there are all those empty rooms.'

A little to her surprise Sybille had agreed without protest. 'If it is no trouble, then I shall be very glad, very grateful.'

'I'll take Sybille to the house,' Roz said quickly. 'You go on to the factory. Pa'll be glad to see you even if it's only for half an hour. I expect you'll be glad to get your head down.' She was making signs at him behind Sybille's back indicating she wanted him to agree.

He glanced at his watch. 'I suppose I could do just that.' He returned to Sybille. 'That is, if you don't mind?'

'Of course. I do not wish to be any trouble, please.'

Roz smiled. 'I'm sure you won't be that. I'll go and get the car if you hang on a moment.' She followed Max down the steps to where his car stood at the kerb.

'Well?' He turned and took her hands in his. 'What do you think?'

She leant forward and kissed him lightly on the lips.

'Things are seldom what they seem; I think a lot of things, amongst them that there is a great deal more to that young lady than might appear.'

Sybille stood at the foot of the stairs. Her thoughts were in a turmoil since meeting Roz. She had come to England, thinking it might at least be possible to take up the threads of the love she and Max had had — that he had been told she was dead, convinced of it, was a traumatic shock with which she had not yet fully come to terms. She had tried now to put herself in Max's place — which wasn't difficult for her love for him was as deep as ever, that was something she knew would never change. But she realised it was not possible to walk back into someone's life, someone who had thought you were dead and who had come to terms with that fact and started his own life anew. She could imagine what that must have been like — knew only too well what it had been like for her, under very different circumstances, granted. But suppose the circumstances had been reversed, had it been she who had thought him dead, would she not too have tried to readjust? Not to forget, that never, but to start afresh — with the memories always there — but life had to go on. Perhaps she, too, would have found someone else to love — although she couldn't imagine such a thing occurring. But men were different — to them love was a thing apart — to a woman, everything.

She liked Roz, no doubt about that, had taken to her at once. That, too, had added to the fact that she simply couldn't expect to walk back into his life as if nothing had happened. She couldn't think why she had really ever thought it would be so simple. But now she knew what had to be done. They must be reassured, she must explain how she felt.

She went down the steps to the pavement where Max and Roz stood by his car.

'I do hope my going to your father's house is not troublesome,' she paused a moment, 'I really feel I am being a burden, that I should not have done this. After all it is time I stood on my own two feet . . . ' She looked down at them, grinning. 'They are large enough, I think!'

The tension was relieved. Roz laughed.

'No bigger than mine . . . but please, don't say such things, it is no trouble at all. Pa will be glad to have your company; it'll stop him nagging me, too!'

Sybille shook her head.

'It will only be for a short time, please tell him that. All I ask is that you bear with me for a little, till I can get . . . how you say . . . set up, established.'

Her tone, her words were so disarming in their simplicity and obvious sincerity, they brought a lump to Roz's throat. She knew Sybille was being completely honest, that she was wholly vulnerable; there was no sign of deviousness in her attitude. She gazed at Roz now from the big, clear, candid eyes, and Roz was reminded of a small child.

With an impulsive gesture she put out her hand, took Sybille's.

'Look, we're going to love having you. It's just that it was a bit of a surprise — all round, I guess — but a nice one. So let's go and get you settled in, we can talk later . . . '

She gave Max a brief kiss and squeezed his hand.

It was difficult not to show too blatantly her delight, her feeling of reassurance from Sybille's words and attitude . . .

9

Edward was out, of course, when Sybille and Roz reached Old House, for which the latter was thankful; in fact she had known he would still be at the factory, and had been anxious, before he returned, to get the girl installed and perhaps changed into some of her own clothes, if she could persuade her tactfully to do so.

Edward after all was a man, and as such was susceptible to immediate impact and first impressions where females were concerned. Roz had no illusions that he was different just because he was her father — and she was anxious now, more than ever, that Edward and Sybille should get on well together.

She wasn't absolutely sure why she was so keen for this to be so, but she had an intuitive feeling it was essential.

Meg was, of course, her usual warm self. She was too tactful to remark on the fact of how ill and old Sybille looked for a young woman in her early twenties, Roz had already been careful to brief her — with as much information as she thought necessary — saying she was an old friend who had had a bad time in East Berlin — she did not specify who was the old friend's counterpart — but she was pretty certain Meg would guess. She was shrewd as well as kindly, and a hard core of north country common sense ran under the kindness.

She had some coffee ready, and said, 'There is hot food if you need it, Miss Roz. I wasn't sure if the lady would have eaten or not.'

Sybille shook her head. 'Thank you, I am not hungry. But the coffee would be lovely.'

They drank it in the drawing room with its white carpet and walls, its Spanish hand loomed rugs in bright colours, with bowls of late spring flowers — hyacinths and narcissi — filling the air with sweet perfume. A fire of apple logs burned in the open grate, and for a moment as she entered the room, Sybille stood perfectly still, one hand to her lips as she had looked round; then she said softly, more to herself than Roz or Meg.

'Beautiful, I had not remembered there was such beauty. Wunderbar — wunderschon . . . '

'Your English is much better than my German,' Roz smiled at her. 'We are very lazy as a nation, very insular still about learning other people's languages.'

'We learn at school of course, and then when I was in prison, for a short time I work in the library . . . ' She paused a moment and her eyes lighted up. 'That was good, I enjoyed it so much. I read a lot — your writers — Hardy, Galsworthy, Shakespeare, and many others, but it was only when I came out of hospital, before I am put to work.'

'I'm surprised at them having books from the decadent Western Kultur on that side of the wall,' Roz said, the words slipping out before she really had time to think, but if Sybille felt any kind of resentment she certainly did not show it.

'I agree, they are a curious people, one would think all their reading would be Marx and his like, but there were many books on science, on electronics . . . ' She paused and dropped her gaze.

'I see.' So that was it, Roz thought, light starting to dawn. But she felt it best for the time not to press the point. This was something that was going to have to be handled with the utmost care and tact, even more than she had envisaged, and perhaps for a very different set of reasons.

She led the way up to the spare room, going first through the door. The long, silken curtains billowed inwards with the early evening breeze, bringing the scent of spring with them from the garden below. A bird sang in the lilac and sunshine slanted through the slats in the blinds, which Meg had lowered so the carpet should not fade.

Dear Meg, she thought of everything, although Roz doubted if there was enough strength in the spring sun to fade the pastel colours of the Chinese rugs.

She turned, hearing a faint sound from Sybille behind her. Once again, the girl stood entranced as she gazed round at the four poster with its damask hanging, the matching covers, the soft white rugs and the dressing table with jars and bottles reflected in the triple, gilt framed mirror.

'This is for me?' Her eyes travelled round the room and finally came to rest on the bed. 'This is a dopple-zimmer . . . '

Fortunately Roz's German was good enough to realise Sybille meant she thought it was a double room — and the implications that went with it.

She went over and took her hand,

'Yes, it is as you say, a dopplezimmer, but that has no significance, I can assure you, it's just that it's the only guest room with its own shower and bath, and I thought you would be more comfortable, more private in that way.'

For the first time Sybille really looked at her full in the eyes, and Roz could see they were beautiful; huge, dark, liquid as of some forest animal, and for a moment they were as she knew they must have been when Max had first known her as a young girl — candid, clear — then once more the shadows filled them, as if she had drawn a curtain, and challenged anyone who might think of trying to penetrate it. But she smiled — at least her mouth did — showing the beautiful teeth that Max had noticed.

'I do not know how to say thank you for all you do — nor do I know why,' she added, her voice a little cooler.

Roz turned away and opened the door that led into the bathroom with its pale turquoise bath and fittings, its matching carpet and towels, even the soap and bath oil toned in with the general scheme.

Sybille was looking over her shoulder. 'Could I have a bath now do you think?' It sounded like a small child asking for a treat.

Roz burst out laughing. 'Of course, be my guest.'

Meg had put the small case on the bed, pathetic amongst all that beauty. The big handbag still hung on Sybille's shoulder, one hand clutching it as though she feared it would at any moment be snatched from her.

She glanced now towards the case.

'I have so very little . . . we are not . . . were not allowed . . . I could not, under the circumstances, bring much with me.' She hesitated, and then as if she had made a sudden decision, said with a kind of endearing frankness, 'I had little to bring.'

Roz smiled. 'I still keep my own room here, my father likes to think I haven't left him entirely! There's a cupboardful of clothes I seldom wear, because they don't fit into my present life style, but to him this means the bird has not actually flown the nest.'

For a moment Sybille looked confused.

Roz laughed. 'Sorry. That's probably a very slang English expression which doesn't translate into German, but it simply means I am still tied loosely to his apron strings — if one can use that for a father as well as a mother.'

Sybille grinned. 'Of course, I understand. You are the only one, I think. And so very precious naturally, is that it?'

'Well, I suppose you could put it that way.'

As she heard the words Sybille had just spoken, Roz realised the tremendous gulf — contrast — between herself, who had everything, who always had had everything — and this girl who had nothing; who once, perhaps, had been cherished and spoilt as she was — and then suddenly lost it all.

The thought, revelation, made it even clearer how she must have felt about coming to England to find Max again. And then to find he had thought her dead, and to have found someone else to love, to marry.

The thoughts racing through her mind made her feel a warmth and compassion for this girl she hadn't even visualised as being possible when Max had first told her about Sybille. She had, of course, intended to be kind, gentle, understanding, but she had not anticipated this uprush of compassion, of deep caring.

'Look, don't be offended, but I really have got stacks of stuff I never use. It's a shame really. Would you like to look and choose one or two things to wear? A dress, some sweaters, a skirt . . . honestly, you'd be doing me a favour. I often have a terrible guilt complex about all the things in there. I'll never wear them all. I lead such a different life now at the hospital.'

'You are a nurse? Max did not say.'

'No, a radiologist; therapy, X-rays, that kind of thing.' She took Sybille's arm. 'Come along, I'll show you some of the things.'

She led the way into her old room. It was just as she left it. Her father insisted it be kept always ready, just in case she should return. But in spite of the fact that she had assured him she intended to keep on her flat, there were fresh flowers, books and magazines — even a bowl of fruit. Yet it had the air of emptiness a room gets which is not lived in. Roz slid back the cupboard doors, revealing racks of luxurious clothes. Sybille gasped; but she slowly shook her head.

'No, I could not, really. They are not my style — you will not be offended, I am sure, but they would look so out of place.' She gave a little gesture indicating her thin body, her rough hands. 'I do have a little money — perhaps we could go to a shop and

I could get one or two things.'

Roz closed the cupboards. For a moment she had been a little hurt that her offer should be refused; but she realised what Sybille had meant.

'Of course. Tell you what, if you like to freshen up a bit, have your bath later, we could go right out and get one or two things before dinner. The shops don't shut till six; there are some quite nice ones in what we call the 'village' nearby. We don't need to go right into town.'

She had said this because she had an account at the little boutique and she felt if Sybille ran out of money, she could more easily help her out there, at least temporarily.

If the girl in the shop was surprised at Sybille's appearance, she was too polite to say so. Roz explained that her friend had come over from Germany without the chance to bring much with her, 'Could we see a few dresses, some skirts and sweaters perhaps?'

'Please, I cannot choose,' Sybille

whispered while the girl held up a silk jersey dress in a pale smoke colour. 'You know so much more than I. Decide for me what is right.'

Roz laughed. 'That dress would be endlessly useful, and that colour would be marvellous. You could dress it up with beads and scarves . . . ' she stopped abruptly. Of course, the poor girl didn't have beads and scarves. How easy it was to forget. She went on quickly. 'That tweed skirt in the check, and then a couple of shirts and a sweater to tone — do you like them?'

Sybille nodded, her bottom lip caught between her teeth. She waited till the girl had gone to fetch some more stock and whispered, 'I do not think I shall have enough. I am not sure how much these are worth.' She held out some five and ten pound notes. To Roz it seemed quite a large sum to be carrying with her.

'Oh, you'll have heaps there, and I'd like to give you a present of a sweater as you won't accept mine.' She laughed.

'As a matter of fact you were quite right, it's just as well you decided not to, now I see the size you take; mine would have hung on you.' Now they both giggled like schoolgirls.

Having had the clothes packed into a box, they put it in the boot of Roz's car. She glanced at her watch. 'Just time to get a couple of pairs of shoes.'

As they walked along the pavement to the nearby shoe shop she stopped before they went in to look at what was in the window, pointing out a pair of sandals and some flat heeled shoes she thought might be suitable.

As she did so, over her shoulder she saw the reflection of a man. Normally she would not have taken much notice, although it was a window full of women's shoes — but this man she had seen before. He had been standing on the corner of the street which led to her flat, when Max had driven off, just before she and Sybille had got into her own car to go to her father's. The reason she had noticed him in the first place was because he was holding a newspaper in front of his face, but he hadn't been reading it; he had been glancing over the top. Also he had been wearing a tartan cap like golfers wear and it had looked totally incongruous somehow. He had turned to the side then, the paper lowered and she had seen he had a black beard, in contrast to which his face was deathly pale. There was no mistaking him.

With a cold feeling along her nerves, she realised they were being followed. She swung round. No one stood there. People hurried by on their way home from work, the pavement was crowded. Whoever it was had vanished among the throng of people. She was sure it had not been imagination. Fortunately Sybille had been too engrossed in the sight of so many pairs of shoes to notice. Now she pointed to a pair at the back of the window.

'Those are beautiful, I think. Real leather. Too expensive . . . '

'Then please let me . . . '

'No.' Her voice was almost shrill. 'No,' she repeated more gently. 'When, as I say, I am established here in England, when things are arranged, then perhaps I can have some of these things, for now, as it is, I am lucky . . . '

★ ★ ★

Back at Old House, while Sybille bathed and changed, Roz went to talk to Meg. She explained a little about the labour camp, bringing tears to Meg's eyes. 'Poor lamb,' she wiped her face with the corner of her apron. She was always deeply moved by cruelty of any kind, specially to children and animals, or the defenceless. It was pretty obvious she had seen through the unnatural ageing Sybille had suffered, for she said,

'She's quite young, Miss Roz.' And Roz knew she meant 'a bit young to be *your* school friend.'

Roz glanced away. 'Yes, she's only twenty-three — it's six years since . . . ' She didn't want Meg to get any wrong ideas, and yet she couldn't lie and say Sybille was an old acquaintance of either hers or Edward's; Meg was too much one of the family not to realise that wasn't true.

'She . . . Max knew her mother when he was in business in Berlin some years ago, and Fraulein Klein thought — you know — she'd like to look him up as she was in England.'

It sounded pretty implausible in her own ears, but if Meg thought so, too, she said nothing. They discussed the menus, as Roz explained Sybille would be staying at Old House for a week or two.

If Sybille had looked in wonderment at the house, it was nothing to Roz's reaction when she saw her half an hour later. She had washed her hair and it shone like burnished silver. She had used some of the make up Roz had put out on her dressing table, and with surprising expertise — understating the gauntness of her features, using eye shadow and shaper so that she had managed to achieve some substance to her face, the cheekbones highlighted.

She wore the silk jersey dress, and although she was so painfully thin, she held herself with grace and poise so that it hung in folds and hid the starkness. She had beautiful legs, encased now in nylon tights, and on her feet a pair of sandals with high heels and ankle straps. She stood in the doorway like an uncertain schoolgirl, not sure whether she would be praised or censured.

For a moment Roz wondered if she had done the right thing for her own peace of mind. When Max saw her now he must realise she still had a bewitching beauty, a honed down finesse which probably was even more attractive than the teenage plumpness had been. There was a charisma, an indefinable quality which was perhaps sex appeal — personality — what you will — something no ill-treatment or starving could quell, instantly recognisable by either sex in the other.

Roz got to her feet.

'You look stunning,' she paused a moment, then smiling, added, 'Wunder-bar!'

Sybille came further into the room. The shoes, the clothes, the added confidence lent grace to her carriage, her head held high, and once again she smiled — dazzling, wide mouthed. Roz felt a further twinge of unease. Had she made a rod for her own back?

She went to the drinks cabinet. 'How about a sherry before dinner? Father won't be long, he likes to eat fairly early.'

'Thank you.' Sybille sat on the sofa, her legs neatly crossed. It was almost impossible to believe this graceful, self-confident girl could be the same person as the crumpled, tired, shabby woman she had appeared at first. It was a complete metamorphosis — the butterfly from the chrysalis.

Roz poured two glasses of sherry into the heavy, cut glass goblets, and carried them over to the low coffee table, sitting opposite Sybille. It was difficult to take her eyes off her, but as the girl stretched out her hand to pick up the glass, Roz thought — that's one thing she hasn't been able to change — the roughness of her hands, the broken nails, and for the first time she noticed the number tattooed on the inside of her wrist.

The stigma that would forever indicate she had been in a communist labour camp . . . and with a little shiver she suddenly remembered the man with the beard.

10

Before she could say any more, she heard her father's car in the drive. She wondered what his reaction was going to be to this girl — this woman. Already it was obvious some of her glamour had returned, perhaps a more mature kind of beauty, not the young, fresh, unspoiled kind Max had known, remembered and spoken of. Her father would be expecting that perhaps . . .

Roz got to her feet, gently pulling Sybille up to stand beside her. She put her arm along her shoulders, feeling their pitiful thiness under the rich fabric of the dress. She didn't know why, but for some reason she felt now she had to protect Sybille, to present her at her very best. It was terribly important her father should like her.

Even in the short time they had spent together, she recognised there was someone very special here; she knew if she could convey this to her father in the first brief encounter, he would accept her valuation without question, which would make the situation much easier for all of them.

The door opened and he stood on the threshold. For a moment his eyes went from his daughter to Sybille. Surprise flickered, but only momentarily. He said slowly, 'I am glad to see you Roz my dear, but I expected to find Fraulein Klein with you. What has happened? Max told me she had arrived.'

Roz smiled and drew Sybille forward, her arm still protectively round her. 'This is Fraulein Klein, Father — Sybille Klein, my father — Edward Henson.'

Again for a fraction of a second he paused; then he held out his hand. 'My dear Fraulein — welcome to Old House, and to England . . . I am so very pleased to meet you.'

As he moved forward Roz saw Max

stood behind him, his eyes taking in the whole scene. They were resting now on Sybille. His jaw had dropped — but whether with surprise at Sybille's appearance, or the fact that the two of them were on such good terms, Roz couldn't tell.

Now that the first few moments were over, and they had gathered round the dinner table, the atmosphere became more relaxed. Edward, who had known Germany before the war — the Germany from which Sybille originally came — kept the conversation going with many reminiscences. He had hunted in the Black Forest, taken the waters at Baden, been ski-ing in the Austrian Alps — all of which Sybille had heard her own parents talking of, although she herself, of course, could not remember it. Their animated conversation left Roz and Max in a contented silence as they ate. Now and then his hand rested on her knee, giving it a little squeeze of reassurance as if he realised how she must be feeling.

After dinner, Meg brought them coffee in the sitting room. Max had put some soft music on the record player and lowered the lights. Edward asked Sybille if she minded his smoking a cigar. She smiled. 'Please do, it will be lovely to smell such a thing again. It is part of the memory, the nostalgia of childhood. More years than I can remember — I have not smelt such a thing — seen such beauty and comfort,' she waved her hand round the room.

They talked of trivial matters now and it was still quite early when Max got to his feet and said, 'If no one else is tired, I am, and I'm sure Sybille must be. I don't seem to have had any sleep since I can remember.' He grinned. 'Must be getting old, there was a time sleep didn't matter.' Roz tried not to notice the glance that passed between him and Sybille and got up, too.

'I have to be early in the morning. Will you be OK, Sybille? Pa's out most of the day, as you know, but Meg will get you anything you want. There are stacks of magazines, and of course the telly or the radio. Pa will show you how they work.'

Sybille smiled. 'Please, not worrying . . . I shall be lovely . . . that is not the word, I think.'

The other three burst out laughing. 'As a matter of fact it's very appropriate,' Edward said slowly, 'although not quite what you meant, I think.'

Sybille blushed. 'Perhaps it would do no harm to study some English grammar, and the dictionary . . . '

Edward nodded. 'Plenty of books in the library, my dear. Help yourself.' He glanced at Max. 'A good idea, specially if you are thinking of getting some employment here. The better your English, the easier it will be.'

Sybille looked down at her hands. There was silence for a moment, then she said, 'Of course. That I must do as soon as I can.' She got to her feet. 'And now perhaps you will forgive if I, too, go to bed.' At the door she paused and looked at the three of them, her face pale again now. 'I cannot thank you all properly for all you have done. One day perhaps I shall be able, and now, auf wiedersehn.'

They heard her heels tapping on the polished boards of the hall, she ran lightly up the stairs. For a moment no one spoke, then Edward said softly, 'I had no idea she would be so beautiful — she is lovely.' He glanced at Max.

He was lighting a cigarette, the flame flared up and reflected in his eyes for a moment and he said softly, 'Nothing like she was. She was breathtaking.'

As if to compensate for his words, he put his arm round Roz. 'Well, my darling, I am so grateful to you for all you have done.' He bent and kissed her on the lips. 'She is like a small child, bewildered. It will take a little while for her to settle, then we must find her somewhere to live, and some kind of a job — unless she wants to return to Germany.'

'I can't imagine she will want to do that,' Edward said, 'unless of course she can stay in the west. I have no idea what the position is, but I have to admit it seems a little odd to me, letting her come out — to find an old flame.'

'She had no idea I thought she was dead,' Max said. 'I suppose it was natural.' He looked at the end of his cigarette. 'Perhaps we would have done the same in similar circumstances.'

'I can hardly imagine an English girl being in the same circumstances,' Edward said.

'That is where we are lucky, but I didn't mean that exactly,' Max said as he went to the door. 'Well, as I said, I'm off to bed. Tomorrow is another day.'

For a moment Roz stood with her hand through her father's arm as they listened to Max's engine die away in the distance. Then she turned and kissed his cheek.

'I wonder what he meant by that.'

Edward shook his head and went to the drinks cabinet.

'A brandy, love? I guess he meant just what he said, that tomorrow is another

137

day, with all its problems — and some solutions.'

'I hope he did.' She paused for a moment. 'I hope he wasn't thinking of John Donne when he wrote, 'Only our love hath no decay; This, no tomorrow hath, nor yesterday, Running, it never runs from us away' . . . at least, if he was, that it was me he had in mind.'

She took the brandy from her father. For a moment his fingers lingered on her hand.

'Don't worry, love. That girl doesn't mean any harm to you, of that I am sure.' He hesitated. 'Blowed if I know what she does mean, quite honestly.'

Later, Roz wondered why she hadn't spoken then to her father of the man she had seen following them . . .

11

After such strange happenings, the next few days seemed to settle into some kind of routine or pattern. Roz went home some evenings when she wasn't going out with Max. Edward had taken an extraordinary liking to Sybille and much to Meg's surprise, came home on time for his evening meal.

On the Saturday evening Roz and Max had been invited to dinner by the owner of a new restaurant he was opening. It was in the country club near the cottage where they intended to live when they were married. Max reminded Roz about the appointment the night before.

'I think I ought to see if I can get another ticket and ask Sybille to go with us,' she said. There was silence for a moment the other end of the phone. 'Are you still there?'

'Yes,' he said slowly, 'perhaps we should. It might be better if the invitation came from you. I'll fix it with Tony.' Tony Stansfield was the club owner.

Roz was taken aback for the moment. Then she realised Max was right. She went over to Old House in her lunch hour. Sybille was in the kitchen talking to Meg, the two had become firm friends and the girl was telling her about Austrian cooking.

'Hi! Sorry to interrupt, but I wondered if you'd like to go out to dinner tomorrow night. It's a new restaurant in an old country house — a club actually. The owner's a friend.'

Sybille smiled. 'You are kind, so kind, but no. I think the quiet life suits me. And Meg — her food is so good I cannot miss one meal of it. I may go into the park to feed the ducks. I see them through the railing yesterday. They are such droll creatures, that I should like.'

Roz laughed. 'Well, I don't know that

Tony would be flattered at the thought of competition to his new restaurant from the ducks in the park — but you could be right. I expect it will be noisy, smokey, and about half way through the evening Max will wish we hadn't come. I'll just give him a ring, he was going to get an extra ticket.'

In a way she had to admit she was relieved. Not because she didn't want Sybille to join them, her company was most enjoyable — she had a quick wit and a good sense of humour — but she hadn't had much time alone with Max since Sybille had arrived, and there were many things they had to talk over . . .

It was odd, but she had known from the outset the evening was going to be a disaster — but quite how much of one, and in what way, of course she had no idea.

She had bought a new dress. Black taffeta with a strapless bodice and straight skirt which showed off her tan and the corn-gold hair to perfection.

Max called for her at eight. The opening ceremony was to be performed by a local dignity at nine.

'We'll need to be a bit mellow if we're going to have to listen to that fellow pontificating,' he had said when he rang to make the final arrangements. Now, as she came down the stairs towards him, he gave a wolf whistle, and a little bow.

'Madam! You look enchanting — magnifique — gorgeous, I don't know how I shall last the evening without eating you.'

She felt a little lift of the heart. The last few days hadn't been easy; although she was sure of his love, his faithfulness, the fact that Sybille was a part of his past, which he had long ago put aside, for which now he only felt a compassion, a warm pity, was something with which she reassured herself. And now, although his words were said lightly, she felt they were sincere. Max was always a man of few words.

Tony had recently been to Corfu, and

had been greatly influenced in his decor by Greece and the islands. The restaurant was decorated as a taverna. The food was to be Greek, and metal jugs of retsina stood on the tables, an olive tree grew in the middle of the floor, and musicians in Greek national dress played bousouki music . . . Max paused a moment at the entrance to the bar.

'Good grief! I fear the worst — ouso and mezes — followed by moussaka.'

Roz laughed and took his arm, leading him to the bar.

'Now, don't knock it. Tony has really made an attractive job of it, and it's better than a Spanish set up. Their food always makes me ill. After all, the Greeks do wonderful salads, and their sweets are gorgeous. If only I wasn't thinking about my waistline!'

Max put his arm round her. 'It's a beautiful waistline, I wouldn't have it anyhow else.'

They managed to get two gins and tonic, and sat at the bar, chatting to

Tony and one or two other of their friends.

'And when is the wedding?' someone asked.

Roz was about to tell them the date when Max got abruptly to his feet and took her arm. 'Come on, love, our table's ready, and I'm starving.'

When they were seated and had given their order, she said quietly, 'Why didn't you want those people to know we're getting married. It's no secret, is it?'

For a moment he didn't answer, then the waiter came with their first course, asking Max about the wine, so that it was a few minutes before he replied.

'Look love,' he said at last, 'we've got lots to talk about, to discuss. Don't you honestly think it would be better just to postpone it for a little while?'

Roz couldn't believe she was hearing right. For a moment all kinds of thoughts went through her head. She was about to explode in sudden rage at such a suggestion, but she bit back the angry words and said coolly, 'I can't honestly say that I see any good reason.'

'Can't you? Be honest. You must be feeling a little confused, the same as I am. I feel I need time to get sorted out. After all, what has happened is of importance, consequence.'

'Not in our lives,' she said quietly, 'at least I didn't think so. I'm desperately sorry for Sybille, but she herself had made it plain she expects nothing from you. To postpone the wedding wouldn't do anyone any good, quite the opposite. Knowing her as I do I think she would be upset to say the least.'

'But I think it would be only polite, kind, not to let her be exposed to our obvious happiness, when her own life is unhappy . . . that is the only reason, honestly Roz . . . I'm only suggesting we postpone it for a little while until . . . well, perhaps until she has settled herself — got some kind of background — established herself, as she put it.'

'Hasn't it occurred to you she may want to return to Germany?' Her voice was so low he wasn't sure if he had heard right. He was just going to ask her to repeat the words when the waiter came to the table.

'Mr Pierce, I am so sorry, the telephone, it is very urgent.'

Max glanced at Roz. 'Who knew we were coming here?'

'Only Pa, as far as I know.'

'My God! This is where I came in, isn't it? What on earth can it be this time?'

'Shall I come with you?'

'No, at least one of us might as well finish our dinner in peace. I'll let you know what it is. Can't be another ghost from the past ... probably something that's blown up at the office. Shan't be long — I hope.'

Roz was filled suddenly with a terrible foreboding; it was so short a time ago just such another telephone call had burst into their lives and changed everything ...

Edward sounded so remote it was like a long distance call. At first Max could make neither head nor tail of what he was saying.

'An accident? You've had an accident? Where are you?'

'No, no, it's Sybille. She's been rushed to hospital. I don't know any details. Could you get there as soon as possible? The police rang me asking for her next-of-kin. I couldn't think of what to do.'

'It's OK. You did the right thing. I'll go right over.'

He went back to the table. Couples had started to dance, the heat was overwhelming. Roz looked up. She was shocked at the pallor of Max's face. 'Darling, what is it? Has something happened to Pa?' She got up quickly and took his arm.

'No, but we'll have to . . . at least I'll have to go. There's no need for you to. It's Sybille. She's been rushed to hospital in Dudhampton. Edward hasn't got any details. The police rang him.'

'Oh, my God! Of course I'll come.'

They didn't talk as Max drove to the hospital, each busy with their own thoughts. Roz was thinking of the man with the beard . . . she had no idea why. Even in the car with the roof open the evening was stifling, thunder rumbled angrily in the distance.

When they reached the hospital she said, 'I'll wait in the car.' She felt at the moment she simply couldn't take any more drama.

The doctor could only tell Max what the police had reported. A man had rung them. He said a woman had collapsed in the park, near the pond where the ducks were. He left no name and the police had had difficulty in understanding what he said; he seemed to be foreign. They had sent for the ambulance. Sybille had been found unconscious. A bystander said they had seen a man sitting on the seat beside her just before she fainted. He had run off into the street . . . it was only because she was carrying a book with Edward's name and address on the flyleaf that they had got in touch with him.

'But what is the trouble? Was it a heart attack?' Max felt more bewildered than ever.

'No. Apart from being too thin, undernourished and anaemic, we can find nothing wrong from preliminary tests. But of course we shall carry out more. It will be easier when Fraulein Klein regains consciousness. In the meantime, Mr Pierce, perhaps you could fill us in with some of the details of her address at home and so on.'

Max couldn't tell them much. He said he understood Sybille had been in some kind of prison behind the Iron Curtain, but they would have to wait for details until she regained consciousness . . .

As they talked, the Sister came to say she had indeed just become conscious. 'If you would like to wait here, Mr Pierce, I will see if it is possible for you to see her for a moment. It will depend entirely on her condition.'

Max went out to Roz. She was pacing the hospital garden, smoking uneasily.

'How is she?' She ran to him. He shrugged his shoulders.

'Can't say. They're going to let me see her in a minute if she's well enough. It seems they can't find anything specific, not yet; they need time.'

Roz nodded. 'Want me to come with you?'

He put his arm round her. 'Better not. Perhaps tomorrow. She must have had a hell of a shock, poor kid, passing out and waking up in hospital.' Slowly he went back into the hospital. As he went through the swing doors the doctor came down the corridor.

'Fraulein Klein tells me she would like to see you, Mr Pierce. But only a couple of minutes, and please, don't excite her.'

She was in a side ward with the curtains drawn. He pulled one back gently and looked at the pale face, the dark shadows like purple thumb marks under her eyes. She had seemed to age again — and yet she looked so vulnerable, so alone, that a great surge of . . . of what? Pity or love or both? Pity was supposed to be akin to love . . . was that simply what he felt?

She turned her head and saw him. Smiling she patted the bed.

'How lovely to see you, and how stupid of me to give everyone so much trouble. You were out to dinner, and I have spoilt it for you and for dear Roz. I am so sorry.'

'Stop apologising for something you can't help, and tell me what happened.'

For a moment she closed her eyes as if she did not wish to face him.

'I fainted. That is all. Just fainted. I guess it is the good, rich food. My poor stomach is not ready for it.' She tried to smile.

'But the man . . . the police said someone reported a man had been seen talking to you, sitting on the seat beside you just before you passed out.'

Her eyes flicked open. For a moment he saw stark, naked fear. It was as if she looked behind him, through him, beyond him at something he knew nothing about. Then as swiftly, she closed them again and said softly, 'What man? There was no man . . . '

12

Max paced the floor of his office like a restless, caged animal. He was conscious of the fact he was doing it and reminded himself of a squirrel he had once seen caught in a trap, actually banging itself against the metal bars until it started to bleed. His case wasn't quite as bad as that; he did have a little control still left, but it was quite impossible to sit still, to concentrate on his work, and heaven knew he had enough on hand. He told himself he should be thankful for it. Henson's Electronics, in spite of the world recession, was flooded with work . . . but all he could see was Sybille's face, the haunted look in her eyes, and hear the words — 'What man? There was no man,' and to know she was lying.

Why? That was the question that kept

going round and round in his mind. Why was she lying?

He walked to the window, unaware that he had done so. He looked down through the dusty glass. The factory was built round a yard, the buildings old, but solid brick. Vans were parked, cars, a lorry stood at the entrance, the uniformed man on the gate was talking to the driver, waving his arms. A young couple — probably from the office block since they did not wear overalls — were standing holding hands, deeply absorbed in each other, oblivious to the outside world. He felt a moment of envy. How simple their world was. He shrugged his shoulders.

'How do I know it is simple?' he murmured out loud. 'Am I being too intense, too dramatic about this whole affair, making a three act drama out of something that can be symplified? But can it? Sybille — she has come through so much . . . suffered more than anyone should have to at her age.'

Now he went back to his desk and sat

down. For a moment he dropped his head on his hands. It was as if the thought of her brought some kind of actual physical pain. Slowly he raised his head. A fly was caught in the window in a cobweb. It buzzed pathetically. The sound seemed to dominate the room. He got up again and went over to it, watching for a moment as it struggled vainly, thrashing about with its legs, its wings pinioned. The spider waited at the side, watching.

With a gesture akin to anger, Max broke the web and freed the fly. For a moment, as if it couldn't realise its good luck, it stayed where it was, trembling, slowly wiping its head with its front legs. Max remembered when he had been a small boy he had laughed once and said to his mother when he had seen a fly doing the same thing, 'Look, Mum, it's knitting'. A brief smile touched his lips at the memory. Then he went slowly back to his desk, sat down and drew out his wallet. Deep in the back pocket was a photograph. He laid it on the desk. It was creased, toffee coloured and faded, but there was no mistaking the girl or her beauty; the bone structure of the face still showed, the sheen of the hair, the whiteness of the teeth.

Beside her stood a younger edition of himself. Slim, his hair blown carelessly in the breeze, wearing an old sweater and slacks. His arm lay along the girl's shoulders. Himself and Sybille when they had first met.

He hadn't even realised he still had it until he had been going through some old papers the other day, looking for something he needed for the cottage. Or had he forgotten? Had the edge of memory nudged, told him that somewhere there was a photograph, somewhere he had it hidden?

He remembered that day so well; it was almost as if he could feel the warmth of the sun, smell the reedy scent of the river. He searched his memory. They had gone on a river trip

— their first outing together. It had been summer, the city hot and dusty, the boulevard cafés were no longer all German, the voices at the tables on the pavement were English, American, Scandinavian.

They had left the car at the landing stage and gone in a motorboat. It had been Düsseldorf. He had had contacts to visit there. The boat had a canopy at the back with a table, and benches to sit on. But they had stayed out in the sun. The boat had been a fast one for its age. He had said, 'This is marvellous. I don't think I really want to do anything for the rest of my life except float along this river with you.' The Rhine, the pleasure boats, Remagen with its neat stone stumps sawn off, and the railway tunnel blocked, suggesting a bridge, without one . . . then he remembered the facts: There was a suspension bridge, it hadn't been blown up and the Americans had used it, but the traffic had been too heavy and it had collapsed. As they went over the spot where the bridge must have disappeared, he wondered what lay beneath the deep water. GI Skeletons, Sherman tanks, and forgotten weapons of war. There were places all over Europe like this, scenes of long ago, sealed off tragedies — just as this one was now, the picture he held in his hand. At the time they had been brought closer together by the disaster. How lucky they had been to survive! Things of the past, scenes now forgotten. What a fickle thing was memory — or was it man who was fickle?

The intercom buzzed. For a moment he had been so drenched in the past, he didn't recognise the sound for what it was. He felt almost light-headed as though he had literally been transported on some time machine.

Edward sounded abrupt, put out, as if he sensed Max's indulgence.

'Max, meet me down in Test Bed II right away, will you? They're about to run advance tests on a new laser

— don't know how Mac gets those chaps to do it, but they're ahead of schedule by nearly a week . . . '

He rang off without giving Max a chance to reply. Or perhaps he didn't expect a reply, instant and automatic concurrence. No, that wasn't fair. Edward was a marvellous boss — would be a marvellous father-in-law.

He put the photo carefully back in the wallet. The pocket was like a secret compartment, you had to undo two straps and a flap to reach it. Why had he buried it like that? A squirrel with its winter store — a memory of summer past.

He went slowly down the iron staircase into the factory. Machinery hummed all round like bees swarming in a lime tree. Now and then someone shouted, someone laughed or swore. Quick footsteps along the concrete floor. A door banged. The smell of a factory, indescribable, unmistakable. Metal, oil, human sweat, dust . . .

Edward was already at the Test Bed.

A man stood either side of him in 'cow' gowns — beige coloured coat-like overalls over their suits. One was Fred Ownes the Chief Technician, and the other Jeff Brinton, Chief Designer. Both brilliant men who, in conjunction with Tony Macdonald, the Chief Engineer, were the backbone of Henson's and had been with Edward since the firm had started. They nodded at Max as he joined them, and went on with the discussion.

'There's been a slight hitch with this model, something to do with the strength of the beam itself.'

Max nodded. It was the project he was particularly interested in, the one used for 'tissue welding' in the medical profession. It had saved eyesight, and lives, the height of sophisticated surgery. At first it had sold mainly to a famous eye clinic in Poland, but as the doctors there had startling results, so the English hospitals had started to use it, and now it was installed in nearly all the ones which dealt specifically with eye problems.

Max turned to Fred. 'Our fault or component suppliers?'

Fred shrugged. 'A bit of both, but thankfully it was discovered on test before the product left these premises. You know Mac; nothing leaves here until it is past the peak of normal perfection, a typical Scot.'

Edward grinned. 'And thank God for the perfectionists of this world. Well, I'll leave that to you two. Let me know how the final tests go. It looks OK to me now, but Mac will have the last word, of course. Now then, I want to know what the progress report is on KL 386. I've seen the analysis graph and the planner in the works office, but I'd like your opinion.'

Jeff nodded. 'I think actually we ought to tighten up security a bit, you know, while we're on the subject. It's not actually my province, but it does seem anyone can wander in and out at will, past the time check office, and this is still on the secret list. I wonder the

Ministry haven't been on our backs already.'

'They have,' Edward said shortly, 'and it's in hand, but it takes a bit of time. Security bods now have to be so screened they go back over five or six generations to see you're clean.' He grinned. 'But seriously I have been putting off calling a meeting and now we must get down to it. The MDD will want to see facts and figures and a practical demo. here in the factory.' He turned to Max. 'Would you see to it? Memo everyone, just say 'cleared for KL 386'.' He glanced at his watch. 'Make it Thursday morning at eleven, that's the fifteenth.' He tapped the calender figure on his watch face with his nail. 'That suit you all?'

Frank nodded, Jeff glanced at the papers in his hand. 'I was going up to York about that steel order, but I don't suppose another day will matter — yes, OK by me then.'

Max turned away, having made a note in his diary, but Edward put his hand on his arm.

'Hang on a moment, I'd just like a word in the office.' He turned and started up the iron staircase. Max had a job to keep up with him. He never ceased to marvel at the other's agility and fitness, and yet he never appeared to make much effort to keep fit. He played golf, but it was spasmodic, he seemed to eat and drink what he liked within reason, and yet there wasn't a spare inch of flesh on him. It was really unfair Max thought; he had to watch his weight, and he found now, at the top of the stairs, he was quite breathless whereas Edward was completely at ease.

Max followed him into his office and Edward waved him into a chair. Lee Firth, his secretary appeared as if by magic with a tray of coffee and biscuits. She put it down on the desk and vanished again. Max stirred his coffee, waiting, expecting Edward to say something about the KL 386, his pride and joy.

'Max, I'm worried,' his voice had an edge to it. Max glanced up quickly, seeing the concern on his face.

'About the project?'

Edward waved his spoon impatiently. 'Good Lord, no, that's as smooth as silk, no much more important to me than that — Roz.'

Max dropped his eyes for a moment. He had to marshal his thoughts, analyse his feelings. He had been away in his mind — so far away in time and place it was difficult to return.

'Her happiness means more to me than anything, I suppose, more perhaps than life itself, although that sounds over dramatic, but it's true nevertheless — and quite honestly I want to know what you are going to do. Oh I know it's awkward for you, damned awkward, I'd be flummoxed in the same position, but it isn't fair on the girl, in fact it isn't fair on either of them, but obviously it's my own daughter I'm thinking of. She is all I have, Max. I was glad when you two came together, it seemed ideal.

Without wanting to flannel you in any way, you are the kind of chap I would have chosen for Roz — and that you are in the business is an added bonus. You're good at your job — and I think you like it or you couldn't do it was well as you do . . . '

Max tried to make some kind of sound of assent. Then he said, 'I know exactly how you feel,' he hesitated a moment, 'the trouble is I'm not sure of my own feelings — no, that isn't absolutely true, I am sure of some of my feelings, but I need time to adjust to all this. It seems to have happened so quickly, and this new development, just when I thought things had sorted themselves out to some extent . . . '

Edward said shortly, 'Things never sort themselves out, my boy, it takes all our own ingenuity to do it for them.'

'I suppose so. But Sybille is due out of hospital any day now. Once we know a bit more about her state of health . . . what she intends to do . . . then perhaps it will be easier.'

He got to his feet. He didn't feel at the moment he could discuss the matter any further . . . he had to be alone, to think.

Edward gave him a shrewd look under his brows. 'It won't be easier, in fact it wouldn't surprise me if it's more difficult, a damned sight more tricky.' He got to his feet as though he also was anxious to close the interview. 'Don't leave it too long, that's all I ask.'

Max turned and went towards the door. When he reached it he hesitated, he wanted to say something, to sound reassuring, to feel reassured, but he couldn't.

Without another word he opened the door and went out. His mind was uneasy, if anything more so than it had been earlier when he had been alone in his own office — alone with his memories . . .

13

Roz insisted on going to the hospital with Max. It had been on the tip of his tongue to suggest he went on his own, but remembering his chat with Edward the day before, he thought it best to say nothing. He still felt the need to be alone with Sybille, and hoped the opportunity would arise, but also didn't want to make an issue out of the matter.

The small white private room was filled with flowers and fruit from Old House on Edward's insistence. Sybille had protested, 'You spoil me to death.'

When they arrived the sister met them at reception. 'I am delighted to be able to tell you Fraulein Klein is well enough to leave, Mr Pierce.' She turned to Roz. 'I am sure you would like a word with the doctor in charge of her case, Miss Henson.'

Roz didn't know quite what to reply. Of course she was relieved at Sybille's return to health, but it had seemed so odd, the suddeness with which she had been taken ill.

'Of course we should, please,' she said.

Dr Franklin was young and very keen on his profession. He carried a clip board thick with sheets of paper, covered with closely written notes.

'It is obvious that for many years the Fraulein has been under-nourished,' he paused, 'or perhaps I should say, eaten the wrong food.' There was a slight query in his tone as he glanced from Roz to Max. Neither of them made any comment. So he continued, 'There is a small scar on one lung, at one time, I suspect, the result of tuberculosis, the other facts also point to this, but it is entirely healed now and nothing to concern ourselves over. I can only think, as she has told me herself, that the sudden richness and perhaps quantity of food she consumed for the first few weeks after her arrival may have upset her. It does happen.' Once again he paused, then he said to Roz, 'Miss Henson, do you think it possible she suffered some kind of shock in the park? I understand a man was seen with her before the police were contacted. Was this someone she knew, or a stranger? Has she spoken to you of this?'

Roz shook her head. 'No, I'm afraid I can't help you.' An utter weariness seemed to fill her these days, since Max had spoken of postponing the wedding. She had tried to be impartial, to do all she could to help Sybille, it was genuine care, for she liked her enormously, but the whole affair had been a traumatic shock, to say the least.

Sybille was dressed and sitting in the day room after they had talked to the doctor. It happened to be empty, her few things were in a case by her side. She got to her feet when she saw them, her eyes on Max's face as she held out her hands.

'It is so good to be up again.' He took her hands in his. For a moment it was as if they were the only two people in the room. Roz stood irresolute, then as if she sensed her feelings, Sybille dropped Max's hands and turned to her. 'It is so good of you to come, to take the time. I could have got a taxi . . . '

'Of course not, I never heard such nonsense. Sit down there and I'll get the car off the park and bring it to the door. I'll only be a few moments, Roz will stay with you.' Gently Max pushed her back into the chair, picking up her case and going out of the room.

For a moment neither woman spoke, then Sybille said, 'He is so kind, so gentle. It is all so ridiculous, that I remember nothing. Only the ducks. They are so comic. They were diving for the bread and suddenly I, too, come over how you say — swimming — everything is going around and I remember no more till I arrive here. I do not know how to thank you all, you are so kind.' Tears flowed down her cheeks now, and before Roz could answer, Max returned.

'The car is out at the front, it isn't far . . . ' the words died away on his lips as he saw her face. He stepped forward and drew her into his arms. 'You are not well, not strong enough . . . ' but she shook her head, pushing him gently away. He gave her his handkerchief, wiping the tears from her cheeks.

'No, really, I am quite all right, it is only this silly weakness . . . '

Roz followed them down the polished corridor, the suitcase in her hand together with Sybille's handbag which she seldom was parted from, but now Max had his arm round her as if she were a small child, half carrying her, her head on his shoulder. It was almost as if Roz didn't exist . . .

Gently he helped Sybille into the back of the car and tucked the rug round her knees. 'Are you sure you're all right?'

'Of course. Please do not worry.' Roz

gave her her handbag. Sybille took it from her with a smile.

'It is heavy, I know, but the reason I cannot be without it, always have it with me — it is all I have to prove my identity, all I have that is me. You understand? My passport, my visa, my identity card, my papers, without them and many other things in there, I am nothing.'

Roz nodded slowly. 'Yes, I understand.' For some ridiculous reason, for a moment, remembering the man with the beard, she wondered if there were a gun in there too . . .

It was only a short drive to Old House. Roz sat silently in the passenger seat beside Max. None of them spoke much, each busy with their own thoughts.

Max drew up in front of the house. Quickly he got out and opened the doors. Sybille was climbing out, then with a little exclamation of dismay, she caught her heel in the hem of her coat. If it hadn't been that Max stood there she would have fallen to the ground. He caught her to him and sweeping her up into his arms, carried her up the steps and into the house.

Slowly Roz picked up the other case and followed them. The ache round her heart was intolerable. Never before had she had to take second place, never before had she felt like an intruder where Max was concerned.

She knew the ghosts of the past were haunting him. Neither of them had discussed the postponement of the wedding any further. It seemed that temporarily Sybille's illness had put everything else into a kind of limbo. But soon she would have to discuss it with him.

Later, dinner over, Sybille in bed, Roz had gone up to her room. Her heart was too full to be with anyone else now. She needed to be alone. Max had had to go to a meeting, and Edward was preoccupied with some papers he was studying.

She had tried to do some ironing.

Her own iron at the flat had given up the ghost and Max had taken it away, promising to mend it and forgotten all about it. She upended the iron and leant her elbows on the board as Meg said, out of the blue,

'That one hasn't had much of a life, Miss Roz.'

Was even Meg in Sybille's thrall? No, that wasn't fair.

'It's more than that, she's under a strain, it's obvious,' she paused, remembering once more the man with the beard, the reflection in the shop window, 'I'm not too sure she's been quite straight with us about everything . . . '

Meg went on chopping herbs for the stuffing she was preparing for the next day. 'Some things are no one else's business, and best kept tidied away.' Her voice had an edge of sharpness and Roz wondered if Sybille had confided more in her than any of them. But, she told herself, the idea was ridiculous — the idea of secrecy — what could there be to hide? She had told them about the prison camp, said her plans were vague, she might return to Germany or she might not.

Now, in the seclusion of her own room, Roz drew back the curtains and looked across the moonlit garden. It was strange that she had been so happy, it had seemed her life was set out before her, as if she could predict the years to come with Max — marriage, children, a stable relationship, a home . . . now all that which had seemed inevitable had become part of a nebulous past, a doubtful future.

Suddenly the whole situation seemed overwhelming. The sobs started some-where deep inside her and welled up so she could not quell them. Scalding tears ran down her cheeks unchecked — she who prided herself on never giving way to such a female weakness. Turning, she flung herself on the bed and abandoned herself to total misery.

She didn't hear the door open, and it wasn't till he sat on the bed beside her that she realised Edward had come into the room. She went into the comforting haven of his arms just as she had as a child.

'Oh, Pa . . . ' the words came out on a hiccup, and she laid her head on his shoulder. The smell of aftershave and cigar smoke wafted her back down the years to the times he had comforted her . . . when she had fallen and cut her knees, when a beloved dog had died, when a kitten had been run over . . . always he had been there to comfort.

Now she said, faltering over the words, feeling some kind of disloyalty, and yet having to utter her thoughts . . .

'I love him so much. And yet I feel it isn't the same. I thought I was so sure of his love, that he felt as I did. Now I don't know any more . . . I just don't know.' He stroked her hair, wondering, searching for words of comfort and reassurance, not even sure if he could give them.

'Look, love, these kind of things

happen all the time in human relation-
ships. It is only something from the past
— something of course he never
thought could happen. He was sure she
was dead. Put yourself in his place,
imagine how he must have felt.'

'It isn't the same,' she said softly,
'loving him is my whole life . . . '

'I know, I know,' he replied, thinking
briefly that if Max had walked in at
that moment he would willingly have
strangled him for causing his beloved
child this anguish. She sat up now and
dried her eyes, trying to smile.

'I'm sorry, Pa, I'm not usually a cry
baby. I must remember I'm a big girl
now!' The sobs were subsiding, but now
and then one rose and wouldn't be
denied, coming out as a hiccup. 'The
trouble is I don't really know how to
handle the situation; I just don't know
what to do. I'm not much good at
feminine wiles, anyway I wouldn't want
him on those terms. I just want him to
love me like he did . . . at least I think
that's how I feel, and then sometimes,

in the middle of the night, or the wee small hours, I wake up and feel so lonely, so cold, and I would do anything, take him on any terms, if only he would come back to me.'

Edward got to his feet. 'I don't think he ever really left you. I think it's just a matter of patience.'

'That's something else I'm not good at!' Roz had gone over to the dressing table and was dabbing at her face, trying to restore the damage the tears had caused. 'He wanted me to go out to dinner, he rang up. But I felt I couldn't eat, be normal in front of other people, so I said I'd meet him at the cottage when his conference is over. I'm going to be entirely female, emotional, remind him of what we had, of all we meant to each other, show him what he's throwing away. I suppose you could say I'm going to have it out with him, although I hate the significance of that expression.'

Edward came up behind her and put his hands on her shoulders, he smiled at her reflection in the mirror. 'That's more like my girl, and luck go with you.' He bent and kissed the soft, shining hair.

14

She drove through the sweetness of the summer evening. Hay lay in the fields as she left the city behind. Wild roses tangled the hedges, and honeysuckle filled the air with its sweetness. Her heart lifted. No one could be entirely miserable in such beautiful surroundings. She thought of the little cottage — it had meant so much, their own home, somewhere they had worked, planned, and loved . . . surely he must feel something of all that.

His car stood outside. For a moment she felt a rising panic, she nearly turned and drove away again, back to Old House, to the comfort of Edward's arms, but it was no use, she had to know, to resolve the situation one way or another.

The door stood open. It was so odd, she hadn't been there since the upheaval of Sybille's arrival. It felt as if she had lived a lifetime since then. The memories crowded back as she stepped into the tiny hall. She had noticed the garden had become quite overgrown since she had weeded it. The weather had been humid . . . the grass needed cutting. The stepladder still stood there where Max had left it that day when the telephone call had come — that first day when the police had wanted to see him. Even the tin of paint, the skin thick on the top, stood on the table, the brush balanced on the edge. The dirty coffee cups, a bottle of milk with the dregs left, sour and yellow in the bottom. The last time she had come down those stairs she had been a different person — light-hearted, looking forward to her wedding, with the man of her dreams in love with her.

Now . . .

She walked along the hall to the stairs. There was no sound. Where could Max be? For some reason she couldn't call his name. She felt to break the silence would be to desecrate it.

Slowly she went up the stairs. The bedroom door was closed. She opened it.

He was standing near the window, silhouetted against the golden glory of the afterglow, his broad shoulders and sturdy frame limned by the light. He hadn't heard her approach. She could see he held something in his hand. But surely it was too dark to read . . . she walked softly across the carpeted floor. As she did so she could see it was a photograph he held. She drew close. She could see over his shoulder now. He held an old photo. A girl and a man with his arm along her shoulders. In the reflection of the sunset she could see it clearly now. There was no mistake. It was Sybille and Max. Her heart lurched. She'd reached the climax, the nadir . . . she knew now, there could be no mistake. He had come here to say goodbye to the cottage and to her. It was Sybille that he loved, wanted, needed.

He suddenly became aware of her presence.

He swung round. 'Darling!' His smile was sad. She could see his eyes still shadowed, only the corners of his mouth trembled. He held out the photograph. 'See what I found? Taken more years ago than I care to think. The years that the locust hath eaten . . . '

He put his arm round her and drew her gently to the wide window seat. It looked out over the garden, where the apple trees cast long shadows in the rising moonlight, to the fields beyond where a tractor still worked with headlights, baling hay. Voices came softly across the darkening fields. Was this going to be the moment of truth? Every detail would be imprinted forever on her mind. She knew that whatever happened, whatever the outcome, she would never forget this moment.

'I've been standing here thinking . . . thinking of the difference, just because Sybille was born a German and we were born English — we are all flesh and blood, people with minds, feelings, emotions, and yet there is nothing in our lives that can compare when it comes to happiness, security, the things we take for granted, things that she thinks of as luxury . . . warmth, enough to eat, security, freedom — yes, that perhaps most of all. Things that you and I take for granted as our right; a shared love, a future, a certainty to some extent. When I think of our happiness, the future we can look forward to for ourselves and our children, then I think of that poor girl, alone, unloved, with perhaps no future, no one . . . '

As his voice died away, she couldn't speak, could hardly think, the relief that flooded through her after the days of uncertainty was like a warm tide . . . and then born on the tide was another flood, of admiration, of love for this man whom she had so completely misjudged, this man who cared, who loved. Once more the tears started in her eyes and ran unchecked down her cheeks as she went into his arms. He stroked the softness of her hair, whispering tenderly in her ear, 'My darling, be patient a little longer, bear with me. I can't utterly reject her, not entirely, not yet.'

Secure now in her new discovered peace and love, she kissed his cheek. 'I can wait, forever if need be, so long as I know you love me.'

He looked at her, 'I don't think you can doubt that, my darling.' The warm tide that rose within her now washed everything else away as his lips came down hard, demanding, on her own, so willing to receive his kiss. And Max, too, felt as if a burden had been lifted from him: he had come to terms with himself at last — but still some of the hardest part was to come, for he would have somehow to tell Sybille there was now no place in his life for her . . . and being the man he was, this gave him cause for great concern.

Now he knew he had to concentrate all his energies on the coming meeting on Thursday which Edward had called on the KL 386 project. Eleven was the time arranged and he had to get to the office early to clear up his outstanding correspondence before the meeting.

The next morning after he and Roz had been at the cottage, with a light heart now, he was just about to leave his flat, his brief case full of the relevant papers which he had brought home to study, when the phone rang. Edward's voice came along the wires more cheerful than he had heard him for a long time.

'Glad to hear you and Roz have sorted things out. I knew you would. After all you're both sane, reasonable folk. It was just what they call a rift in the lute. I'm very pleased it's all cleared up, my boy. Now the purpose of my call is to say I've forgotten to bring some material from my desk at Old House for the meeting this morning. Must be old age, getting senile . . . can you possibly pick it up for me on the way? I've got plenty to get on with here, but those notes are vital. Careless of me. Good thing there's no members of the KGB about, eh? Mind you, I feel pretty stupid having left classified material lying around, but I reckon dear old Meg would guard it like a bulldog if anyone tried to pinch it. Still no one would imagine anyone could be so careless as to leave it lying around. Guess we'll have to tighten up after the Ministry bods have been. Sorry to trouble you.'

'That's OK. Shan't be long.'

He felt relieved Edward sounded in such good form. He whistled as he drove through the warm, scented summer morning. Life was good again.

The front door stood open. Probably Meg was in the garden picking flowers before the sun got on them.

He ran lightly up the steps. No sign of Sybille. Perhaps she was having a late morning in bed, the doctor had said she must still take it easy. He went across the hall to Edward's study door, his feet made no sound on the thick pile of the carpet.

He threw open the door.

At first he simply couldn't believe what he saw. It was like some evil dream. Then he thought perhaps he was mistaken, that there was some perfectly simple explanation. He must have made a slight sound for Sybille swung round. For a moment neither of them moved or spoke. The desk was open and in her hand she held a sheaf of papers. Max knew at once what they were, what information they held.

Her face was a mask of horror, of terror. She burst into sobs that wracked her body as he stepped forward into the room.

15

As Max stepped forward his first reaction at seeing Sybille standing there with the secret papers in her hand, was anger. An anger that could possibly have erupted into violence. Anger with himself for being duped, made a fool of; anger with her for going into the whole thing in such an inept manner, bungling so that he had caught her red-handed.

But as suddenly as it had arisen, the fury subsided as he watched the tormented figure. She sank into a chair, the papers dropping from her hand, scattering on the floor in confusion.

Automatically he bent down and picked them up, scanning them as if it were imperative. Although his eyes didn't register the contents, he knew well enough what they were. It was so painfully obvious — almost a physical pain, that she was a complete amateur, so unskilled in fact it was laughable.

Was it money she had been after? Was she just a common thief short of cash? He dismissed that idea as soon as it entered his mind. That was more impossible than the other idea.

Her collapse into the chair had been because her legs had simply folded under her. She had hidden her face in her hands, a little whimpering sound as a trapped animal might make at the end of its tether, escaped her. He tried to harden his heart — he must harden it.

'What on earth do you think you are doing?' The words sounded a cross between melodrama and the banal. Quite simply he hadn't known what else to say.

Slowly she lifted her raddled face and looked at him. 'I had a phone call . . . '

'Go on, a phone call. From whom, what about?'

She shrank back as if the ice in his tone were a physical thing. He made himself refrain from trying to help her.

She let out a long, shuddering breath.

'This man — I do not know his name — it is obvious it is the same one who came to me in the park — he rang about half an hour ago, soon after Edward had left . . . ' She swallowed the constriction in her throat. Without saying anything he went to the drinks cabinet and poured two glasses of brandy. Briefly, he thought he had never drunk such a thing at nine o'clock in the morning before.

She sat now, her teeth chattering, her whole body shaking. He handed her the glass. At first she turned her head away, unable to look at him.

'Come on, it may help, and you have to talk.'

Slowly she turned her head again, her face now inscrutable, the tears still streaming from her eyes as sobs shook her body. The air between them was tense as if each suddenly felt the other to be a total enemy.

He knew she was hurt, but there was nothing he could do about it.

'Go on, this man rang you.'

He said, 'You are alone, now is your chance. Take it.'

'I see, your chance to take the designs, the drawings of the new laser KL 386, that's it, isn't it?'

He said the words with great deliberation as if he wanted to burn them into her mind, to make sure they were right, that there was no mistake.

'Yes . . . '

He grinned, a travesty of a grin for the movement of his mouth didn't reach his eyes.

'Actually, they are useless to you, these particular papers. They are so arranged, the plans, the drawings, that it would be almost impossible to put them together without expert knowledge. You wouldn't know what to take to make a satisfactory whole.' He paused now and finished the rest of the brandy at one gulp. It was neat and stung his throat as it went down. For some reason he welcomed the discomfort it brought. 'But that is beside the point, isn't it?'

She let out a long, shuddering sigh. 'It is such a long story — so — how you say, ordinary in some ways to people like me, and yet when it happens to you — not ordinary at all. I explain so badly.'

At that moment the phone rang. Max guessed it would be Edward, impatient, wondering what on earth had delayed him. He glanced at his watch. It was only half an hour since he had left his own flat — a half hour which had changed the whole world in some ways.

He lifted the receiver.

'Max? What the devil has happened? Have you forgotten where to look for the papers? We're all waiting.'

'Look, Edward, something's happened, something that can't wait, that even the conference will have to be shelved for.'

Edward started to protest, 'I've got everyone here, even the Ministry bods are coming later. I can't possibly postpone — '

'I think when you know why I am asking, you will come. You will have to trust me. I can't possibly explain over the phone. Could you give Roz a buzz and ask her to come over from the hospital as well? It'll come better from you than me . . . '

'Roz? What the hell has she got to do with it? You know this is her busy time, her assistant is away. Have the papers been stolen or something, or is the place on fire?'

'No, well, not exactly. Look, I know it sounds crazy, but you really will have to trust me, and please come as quickly as you can, it is almost a life and death matter.' He wasn't quite sure what had made him say that. He could tell Edward was put out, to say the least, by the way he banged down the receiver. Sybille was staring at him. There was fear, almost terror, in her eyes, like a hunted animal.

Max turned on his heel. He couldn't speak for the moment, didn't want to commit himself in any way until

Edward arrived — and Roz — somehow it was almost more important to him that she should be there than her father.

He went through into the kitchen. He hadn't had any breakfast. He asked Meg to bring a tray of coffee.

'There's been a bit of a change in plans. Mr Hanson is coming back to the house and Miss Roz. Would you make sure we're not disturbed once they arrive? No phone calls, nothing . . . '

She gave him a curious look, but it was not in Meg's nature to question.

'I'll make the coffee and bring in some cakes — Miss Roz's favourite — chocolate. I don't suppose she had any breakfast,' she said, a note of reproof in her voice. 'High time she had someone to look after her.'

Max went back into the drawing room. Sybille sat as if she awaited the verdict of a court. She had been to her room while he was in the kitchen, washed her face and combed her hair, dabbed at her eyelids with cold water.

There was the sound of Edward's car in the drive. He drew up sharply with the rattle of gravel. Max could tell he was angry at having his plans upset, and would want a first class reason why. Almost at the same moment, with relief, he heard Roz's Mini. Doors banged, voices drew near, the front door was thrown open and Edward came into the room. Roz was close behind him, looking with curiosity over his shoulder, wondering what all the fuss was about, and like her father, annoyed at being dragged away from an important case. But her father had sounded as if it really were serious, although he had told her no details.

'I'll tell you one thing, if it's some kind of wild goose chase, I'll have that young man on toast.' But Roz knew it wasn't likely Max would have taken any steps that weren't essential.

Edward stopped abruptly on the threshold as Max had done, gazing from him to Sybille. She had got to her feet, and said without preamble, 'He ... Max ... found me at your desk with those papers,' she gestured towards the sheaf of papers which Max had put neatly on the coffee table. For a moment it was as if the breath had been knocked out of Edward.

'You're not serious. Surely I haven't been dragged all the way here ... '

With unaccustomed bravado she broke in, 'I think perhaps I have never been so serious in my life.'

'Do you mean to tell me all these weeks you've been living a lie with us, spying?' He almost spat out the word.

'Yes.' It was unequivocal.

'But why? From personal choice?'

His voice, too, was ice cold. He was as furious as Max had been, and as baffled.

She nodded, then shook her head, not sure to which question she was replying, utterly confused.

Edward started to pace the room like a caged animal. Roz had moved towards the fireplace, one arm stretched along the mantelpiece as if she needed support, her eyes on Max, questioning, uncertain.

'Then I think you had better start at the beginning, hadn't you?'

'I suppose you could say I came here under false pretences . . . but you have to believe they were not my false pretences . . . ' her voice broke for a moment; she dabbed at her lips with her handkerchief, and then went on, 'I did come to see Max — I did hope in some wild way to take up again our relationship. By wild I mean perhaps unsure, hopeful, uncertain.' She hesitated again and looked round at them slowly, then she went on in a low voice, hardly above a whisper, 'But please, this I must just say, to you all, I have to say how grateful, how truly grateful from the bottom of my heart I am, for your kindness, your thoughtfulness.'

Edward gave a snort which Max knew boded no good.

Now Sybille turned back and looked at Max. 'Always you were like that, kind. When I got here I found that things — the situation — was not as I expected. Whether the KGB knew the position I do not know. I think it unlikely perhaps. I can only suppose they didn't care. I was released from prison in the normal way. I had served my sentence. They let me go to the West. I had said I wanted to come to England. For some little while they made me stay in West Berlin. I thought there must be some reason. It is all so strange there ... two million people ... ' She seemed now to have gathered a little strength, it was as if she had become unaware of her listeners.

To begin with, Edward had fidgeted, lighted a cigar and then left it in the ash tray, straightened the clock on the mantelpiece, but as Sybille went on talking in her low, rather melodious voice with its accent, he seemed to become suddenly interested.

'Two million people, surrounded by a wall eleven feet high. You cannot imagine it if you had not seen it. Three thousand British soldiers and their families . . . it is their home. Some of them I got to know, it is like an island community, captive yet free. You can get to the city by road, by train — there are air corridors, tightly controlled by the Russians, used by the Allied Forces to maintain their own sectors of course, but only they may use them.' Again she paused, then said, 'You cannot fly Lufthansa to Berlin . . . '

Max broke in now with a touch of impatience.

'Yes, we know all this, but what has it to do with you?'

'There are people called Exfiltrators.' For once she ignored Max and went on as though she had not heard him, 'They are an SAS type organisation, I suppose that is how you would describe them. They demand a high price for their services to Berliners in the East wanting to get out. A sum of thirty thousand pounds was paid lately for a family of three.'

Now she looked down at her hands.

'My mother is still in East Berlin. She is ill, needs special treatment which can only be given in the West. Some people I got to know, they said they would arrange for me, to get her out, but it would cost money, much money, a fortune. I came to England thinking there might be some way I could get help. Perhaps from you . . . ' She glanced at Max for a moment. 'I do not really know what I thought. I was confused, desperate, you seemed like my only sheet anchor.'

She looked away now, her voice low as she went on, 'When I got here the KGB came to me with this proposition — how much they knew of what I was thinking of doing for my mother I do not know, how much my release from East Berlin had been engineered with just this in mind, too, I do not know. But I was told to carry on and see you. Then to get these plans of this laser. They would pay me a large sum of money into the bank in West Berlin.'

Max said slowly, 'It is unbelievable.'

She nodded. 'There is much about Berlin which is like that — a nightmare. The West Berliners have big cars, flashy clothes, they live it up, as you say. They know the Russians could come across any day. Every minute is lived as though it were their last. This feeling, this apprehension in the atmosphere, in the very air you breathe, it is catching. But when they offered the money I needed, I could not refuse.' She stopped and once more looked slowly round at the three pairs of eyes fixed on her. She made a little gesture of helplessness as if asking for their mercy. 'Could I?'

Edward said, 'So now the KGB are pressing for this information?'

'Yes. All the time I am under surveillance, obvious from the phone call. This house even is being watched. In the park, there was this man of course, although to you I had to deny it. He told me if I did not get this information quickly my mother would die.' She turned her face away from them. 'I love her. She is all I have.'

And now Max spoke. 'Will you leave us for a little while, Sybille? We, too, have had a shock from what you have told us, from what you have done. We must have time to talk about it, to decide what steps to take. You understand?'

She got up and went towards the door. 'Yes, of course I understand.' For a moment she hesitated, then she turned and said, 'Whatever you do decide — I repeat, whatever — I will accept it. You have been so kind, I cannot do otherwise.' She went swiftly now as if anxious to get it over with. There was a silence as they heard her light footsteps go on up the stairs, a door opened . . .

At last Edward said, lighting another cigar, 'Well, and what is our verdict?'

Roz shrugged her shoulders. 'It's hardly a verdict. She's guilty, she admits it. But whether we think it is her fault, decide to hand her over to the authorities, that's something else.'

Now she went over and put her arm

through Max's. 'Actually,' she went on, 'I'm only an ignorant woman, I don't know about these things, these secret weapons — but as far as her story is concerned it seemed to me so simple, so naïve I don't see how she could have made it up.'

'Don't be taken in by that,' Edward said shortly. 'That is part of the trick, the innocent bit.'

Roz loosed her hold of Max and went across to her father, who now stood in front of the fireplace, his hands clasped behind his back.

'I don't think it is a trick, not where she is concerned. After all I suppose I've been alone with her more than either of you,' she stopped a moment and glanced briefly at Max, 'at least while she has been in England, and one woman usually can see through another pretty quickly. I admit I didn't realise we were being watched, I admit I never had any suspicions about her, but I just don't think she is the kind of person who would have done all this willingly

'. . . I believe what she says about her mother, I think the poor woman is desperate, perhaps even at the end of her tether.'

'So what do we do?' Edward asked.

'That's something I can't answer. But as she hasn't actually got the papers and now hasn't a cat's chance in hell of getting them, there isn't any harm done. I think we should have her back, tell her we believe her story. We don't much like it, but we'll accept it, and there are one or two points we'd like cleared up.'

Edward studied the end of his cigar. 'Well, I suppose I'm willing to do that. I can't say I like it, the whole thing stinks, and I only hope the Ministry don't find out what's been going on.'

All this time Max hadn't spoken. It was as if he were miles away. Now he said suddenly, 'I'll go and see her, tell her.' He seemed to have something bothering him. He ran up the stairs, two at a time. Her bedroom door was ajar. She hadn't heard him come. She stood with her back to him, looking out of the window. Her shoulders were hunched, she looked vulnerable, beaten. As he watched, she took something from the pocket of her coat. For a moment the light caught it, glistening on a small glass bottle ... he threw open the door and she swung round. He strode across the room,

'Are you OK?' as he spoke he snatched up her hand and forced open the fingers. They held a small bottle of blue pills. He took it and slipped it into his own pocket.

'You won't need those,' he said. 'Come along, the others want to ask you one or two questions. You need not be frightened.'

Roz came to meet them as they entered the drawing room and took Sybille's hands in her own. 'Why go back to Germany?' she said.

Slowly Sybille shook her head. 'You are kind, wonderful, but that I have to do because of my mother.' She hesitated. 'There is a little more I would like to say, please.' She looked at Max. 'The motor cyclist — the messenger sent to the Wall, it was arranged as far back as then, I think, for he was to tell you I was dead with all the others, but already they knew I was not dead. Badly injured, but I had escaped death. This they knew. This they would one day use. Perhaps at the time they did not realise the whole potential, how exactly they would use me — and you — but always they have plans, projects, uses for everything. Never mind at the time, like you do not throw away the ends of candles in case you can melt them down to use again, they kept me, to melt me down indeed.' She gave a little shudder. 'And then in the course of time the use became obvious, as they knew it would. I did not exactly escape from the camp, I was allowed to go, things were made easy, you understand? But I am perhaps the most inefficient, useless spy ever, yes?' She gave a faint, wintry smile. 'There is a little more now, then I am finished. One day soon I shall receive postcard addressed to Max's home — it was the only address I knew to give to the partisans, the people who are helping me in the East Germany. There are those who will help, if the message is the right one, then it will mean my mother is in the West — if not, then there will be no hope for her escape.' She turned back to Roz. 'There is one thing I want you to promise, that you will go ahead with the wedding as soon as possible, please; to put it off longer makes me feel worse.'

Roz glanced at Max, giving a little nod of her head, then she said, 'Perhaps. But at the moment it can wait.' She felt a new confidence now with the reassurance of Max's love, which she had had confirmed so overwhelmingly at the cottage. She went once more and put her arms round Sybille.

At last Edward spoke, turning to Max. 'Well, I think it is about time we went back to work . . . '

Sybille looked at him. 'Are you going to the police?'

He smiled for the first time and put his hand on her shoulder. 'No, my dear, I am not going to the police.'

Impulsively she reached up and kissed him gently on the cheek.

16

It was only a week later the postcard arrived, a brightly coloured picture of the Berlin Zoo, addressed to Fraulein S. Klein.

Max turned it over in his hands. His German was not good enough now to understand the fine writing. He had no idea whether it carried news of life or death for Sybille. For a long time he stood staring down at it, then with a little impatient shrug of his shoulders, he got into the car and drove round to Old House.

Edward and Sybille were at breakfast. Without preamble Max held out the card. Sybille took it quickly without looking at him. For a moment, as she read it, it was as if the film in a camera had stopped, the ticking of the clock on the mantelpiece seemed to fill the whole room with sound, somewhere a door banged, a dog barked, a car started up, someone laughed. Then at last she raised her eyes and looked at him, her lips curved in a smile.

'It says '*Wish you were here*'. It is good news. My mother is free.' She jumped to her feet and flung her arms round Max. 'Now you and dear Roz can go ahead with the wedding at once . . . and I shall go back to West Berlin to my mother.'

Edward, too, stood up and held out his arms. 'My dear, I am so pleased for you. It is the best news we have heard. Max, go and ring Roz and tell her. There is much to be done, arrangements to be made.'

For a moment Max stood irresolute, then he took Sybille's hands in his, making her look at him. 'You are sure?'

She smiled at him. 'Of course. Isn't it wonderful? I shall be able to build a new life, to start living in West Germany, among the friends I have already made . . . and my mother. We shall be able to have a little car, to go out into the countryside which she loves so much . . . it is wunderbar!'

Max went to the phone and rang Roz. 'Darling, we can be married now, just as soon as you can arrange it. I love you . . . '

* * *

It was September. Originally of course they had planned a summer wedding, but the weeks had passed in uncertainty until now. Much furniture had arrived at the cottage; it still stood in its packing cases for Roz hadn't had the heart to unpack it. Now all was feverish activity. They had decided now on a quiet wedding. 'Just family and a few close friends,' Roz put her arm along Max's shoulders. 'I'd awfully like Sybille to be bridesmaid. She hasn't to go back just yet, the arrangements aren't complete. Do you think she'd agree?'

For a moment Max was a little taken

aback; not that he could see anything against asking Sybille to fulfil such a role, in fact he thought probably she would be overjoyed, it was just that women never ceased to surprise him. Only a little while ago he knew Roz thought his old love for Sybille had burst into fresh flame, unsure of herself and him, but now she was prepared, willing in fact, to have that same girl as bridesmaid at her wedding . . .

But he just said, 'Of course, why not? Choose something nice for her to wear and let that be the bridegroom's present to the bridesmaid, eh?'

She kissed the lobe of his ear. 'Good thinking . . . '

They decided on the little church at Badger's Holt. They had been going to be married in the big parish church in Dudhampton — but somehow both of them felt now they wanted something smaller, more intimate. It was as if the traumatic nature of Sybille's visit had had some kind of effect on their relationship, making it more mature, almost as if they were already married, a depth of feeling and meaning far beyond its original state.

'It's funny,' Roz said one evening at the cottage when they were doing the final touches, putting up curtains, arranging books and the other bits and pieces. 'I feel somehow quite different from the person I used to be. I don't know how or why exactly . . . '

He put his arms round her and pulled her down on to his knee, kissing her gently on the lips, making the warm desire flare inside her.

'I do. It's because we have weathered a storm, a pretty fierce one at that. It's hardly likely we shall have to face anything much more traumatic in the years ahead. Crises of course, we all suffer those, the rich fabric of life as someone once called it, but we have come through this one more sure of each other than ever before.'

She got up suddenly. 'You say that, but I have to be truthful. I did . . . well, have some pretty hairy moments . . . '

'I know,' he said quietly. 'It has to be one of the worst situations anyone can be called upon to face, but I'd like you to know there never was a shadow of doubt in my mind, darling. It was just this terrible feeling of guilt in a way, and pity, compassion. They say pity is akin to love, but it wasn't so in this case, at least not in any way that threatened our love.'

She went over to the window, looking out at the beautiful autumn colours, gold, scarlet and crimson against the clear blue of the September sky. She turned back to him.

'I know that, and in a way it makes me love you even more,' she grinned. 'I remember when I was at school we learnt that poem, how does it go? You know, the one by Lovelace, *To Lucasta Going to the Wars*,' *'I could not love thee, Dear, so much, Loved I not honour more.'* I know now what it means. When we were kids we thought it referred to some lady called Honour More! But now to me it means the way you felt about Sybille — and so I love you for it.'

★　★　★

It was a picture book September day — the day of the wedding. The little country church was full of autumn flowers, chrysanthemums, dahlias, Michaelmas daisies and hot house lilies from Old House. It was as warm as summer as Sybille stood waiting in the porch for Roz to arrive. Her face and figure had filled out a little since she had been at Old House, and although she was still painfully thin, Roz had helped her to choose a dress in a deep cream which showed off the tones of her hair and skin. Meg was resplendent in a blue suit which matched her eyes, filled now with tears for Roz had been much like her own child all the years she had worked for Edward.

People crammed the pews and overflowed on to the path outside. The choir boys, brushed and polished like rosy apples, sang 'Morning Has Broken' as the anthem, and Edward stood now with the sun shining through the stained glass of the window. It cast lozenges of purple, scarlet and emerald green on the silver of his hair. He was content now; all the problems seemed to be solved and Roz had never been so happy. Max had behaved in exactly the way he should have over the whole affair. Had he had a son of his own he couldn't have wished for one better . . .

There were many tears shed in the little church that day. The door stood open to the warm late summer sunshine with the sound of one belated combine harvester clacking its way round a distant cornfield . . . tears of joy, of sorrow, of regret . . .

But back at Old House, where a big marquee had been set up on the lawn, everyone was in party mood. Edward stood up to toast the bride, to make his speech. There was a lump in his throat as he looked at Roz, so beautiful, so like her mother had been when they were married. He had made a few notes on a piece of paper, but the words blurred before his eyes.

He took a sip of champagne.

'My friends,' he said then, 'I suppose this is one of the saddest, and yet the most joyful days of my life — sad because I have to hand over my most precious possession — if she doesn't mind me referring to her as that!' He grinned at Roz, she blew him a kiss from the palm of her hand as she had done as a child, and he went on, 'But the hands into which I put her are all I could have asked for. I have known Max for many years, as a friend and business colleague. Had I had a son of my own I couldn't have wished for better. I don't think any father can say more than that . . . ' There was a round of applause.

'What can one say on an occasion like this except to wish them every possible happiness, a long life and to repeat what was said to me at my own wedding.' He paused for a moment, quite overcome with emotion, and then went on, 'The priest told us he was not going to preach a long sermon, simply to say, 'You will have differences in life, it is inevitable, but whatever they may be — big or small — agree to differ. If you think about those words you will realise they cover all the essentials of a happy, unselfish life — and more than that I cannot wish for Roz and Max . . . please join me in a toast . . . God bless them both.'

He sat down, wiping his eyes as he looked at Roz, smiling, happy, carefree. Then he glanced at Sybille. She sat with her eyes downcast, her lower lip caught in her teeth. For a moment sorrow seemed to sit like a dark shadow about her, but as if she was conscious of his eyes on her, she glanced up quickly with a wide smile, waving her fingers at him, lifting her glass and draining the bubbling, golden liquid as if she hadn't a care in the world. She must feel some regrets, he thought to himself, poor kid, still I'm glad everything has worked out so well for her, and with her looks, she'll soon find a young man of her own . . .

Now conversation buzzed. People milled around the tent, chatting, eating, laughing, and Sybille had been drawn into a little knot of people who were asking her about Germany, where they were going on holiday.

Edward stood near, listening to her description of the Germany she had known as a child, the forests, the castles, the Rhine. 'It was a fairy tale country then,' she said slowly, looking almost like a child again as she remembered, her face vivacious, animated.

At last it was time for the bride and groom to leave. They were going only as far as Devon for a brief honeymoon. Project KL 386 had suddenly become of prime importance to the Ministry, and to Henson's Electronics, and Edward had said he could only spare Max for a few days.

'When the whole thing is sewn up, and the bods at the Ministry satisfied, then you can go away for the prescribed month — I've told Roz that is to be my real wedding present to you. A month in any part of the world you like to choose.'

Max grinned. 'I should think you've given us enough already, furnishing the cottage, on top of everything else, but it sounds a marvellous suggestion.' He pressed Edward's arm. Neither of them were prone to much show of emotion, to wearing their hearts on their sleeves, but for a moment the barriers were down as he said, 'Thanks, Edward, for everything.' His eyes were on Sybille as he spoke, standing now on her own, her eyes thoughtful, distant, 'Not least for the way you handled what I can only describe as an almost impossibly involved situation. I think both Roz and I will be grateful to you for that alone for the rest of our lives. One wrong move on your part, and the whole thing might have blown up into something else.'

Edward grinned. 'You didn't do too badly yourself, old son.' He broke off, laughing. 'I hadn't thought when I used that term — but that's just what you are now — son.'

For a moment Max felt a great tide of pleasure. He knew the words had meant much to Edward to say, he never spoke lightly or flippantly, and he couldn't have paid him a greater compliment.

The blue and golden weather followed them to Devon. They ate, slept, made love and walked the moors; basked in the sun and swam in the clear water, which still held the warmth of summer.

On their last morning Roz said, 'Just as well we go back to the everyday world tomorrow, I'm getting fat as a pig with all this food, and loafing around.' She stood before the long mirror, her naked body tanned to a rich gold. Max stretched luxuriously on the bed. 'A life of luxury, of laziness is lovely for a few days, but I don't think either of us could stand it for long. We are a pair of doers . . . just as well perhaps.'

He rolled off the bed and came up behind her, putting his arms round her, cupping her breasts, with his hands, feeling the firmness of her flesh, nuzzling her neck.

'Come back to bed, woman. It's only seven of the clock, and it's the last morning we shall be able to indulge ourselves as the great loafers.'

She needed little persuasion. The early morning sun shone through the slats of the shutters, motes of dust dancing in its beams, as she went once more into his arms.

'I feel positively decadent . . . and I love it,' she murmured in his ear.

17

The weather broke as they drove back to the Midlands. Roz rested her head on Max's shoulder.

'Its only as it should be. The skies were weeping at our return from paradise.'

They were to stay the night at Old House, a final dinner party before Sybille returned to Germany.

Edward welcomed them at the front door. 'My goodness! You two look as if you've been abroad in the sun. I shall have to think of qualifying my offer of a month anywhere in the world, it seems Devon has treated you well.'

Roz went into his arms, laughing up at him, joy spilling out of her as he held her close for a moment.

Sybille waited in the drawing room, not wanting to intrude on the family reunion. Because of the cold greyness of the evening, Meg had lighted a log fire, the flames dancing up the chimney, reflecting from the brass and silver on the shelves.

Roz gave a little sigh of contentment. 'My cup runneth over — honestly it does,' she laughed.

Edward poured the drinks.

'Well it's all fixed up, Sybille's flight, Heathrow on Friday. I thought we might all go down and see her off. Airports are miserable places and it's nice to have friends to wave you off.'

Max went over and sat beside Sybille on the sofa. 'That's a first class idea.' He turned and looked at her now, taking her hands in his. 'You are absolutely certain about this, aren't you? That there's nothing we can do? That the KGB can't make things bad for you again?'

She looked back at him, her eyes steady, then she said, 'Of course, it is all fixed. You saw the postcard.'

He nodded. 'I know, but you must

remember my German isn't all it might be.'

She smiled. 'Then you will just have to trust me . . . ' As she said the words her face clouded for a moment as she thought of what she had been doing when Max had caught her at the desk — far from justifying trust . . .

The rest of the evening passed in general conversation, in descriptions of the wonderful week Roz and Max had had, at laughing over instant photos they had taken. If Sybille was a little quiet, they thought it only natural; she didn't have a chance to say much.

At last Roz said, 'Why don't you bring your mother over next year if she's strong enough. We could all go down to Devon for a couple of weeks, take a house down there perhaps.' Then she laughed and said, 'Oh no, that's not at all a good idea. If we go we'll live it up in the lap of luxury in the best hotel, not with the girls having to do the cooking and the washing up.'

Max waved his hands in mock

desperation. 'I like the idea of the house, no dressing up, no being tied to meal times.'

'Ah, but that's just what we like,' Sybille joined in now, 'the dressing up. Do we not Roz?'

'Of course, and to be pampered for a little while. We'll fix that, it's a super idea.'

By Friday the weather had changed again, the sun shone in a St Martin's summer, as Meg called it.

They drove south, Edward drove the Jag and Max sat beside him, Roz and Sybille in the back. Earlier Max had said, 'She could have flown from Birmingham airport . . . ' Edward had nodded. 'I know, but that's why I insisted on making the arrangements rather than letting her. I thought it might soften the parting a little if we had a trip, all of us, with her . . . '

Max had nodded slowly. There were things he had learnt lately about Edward which he hadn't known about . . . his thoughtfulness, gentleness; it was somehow as if Sybille had come as a kind of catalyst among them.

They didn't talk much now. At first they chatted about the countryside, about the weather, about the wedding, and how Roz and Max were settling into the cottage, but as they drew near the suburbs of London, they grew silent, the talk was desultory. *'Parting is such sweet sorrow'*, the words came unbidden into Roz's mind.

There was just time for a coffee and a sandwich in the lounge. Then Sybille's flight was called.

They went with her to the departure gate. Roz kissed her, squeezing her hand.

'Don't leave it too long before you come back to see us.'

Then it was Edward's turn. 'Send us a card — a picture one to tell us how things are, in English please . . . ' She clung to him for a moment, then Max drew her to him. Her lips were soft as he touched them with his own, for a moment he was filled with a kind of coldness, as if an icy hand had touched him. An apprehension of inevitability, a poignancy the situation didn't really warrant. Her mother was free, she would never have to go to East Berlin again, medical treatment of the right kind would probably make her well again. Wonderful things could be done these days, and Germany had a high reputation for excellence in medicine.

Why should he feel thus? It was as if, as he used to say as a child, a goose had walked over his grave . . .

Then she was gone, a slim, lonely figure, turning once to wave. She looked so vulnerable . . .

★ ★ ★

She had never cared much for flying. Perhaps it was memories from the past days when she had been with the partisans, dropping by night, with a parachute into thick, black darkness, not knowing what waited below.

Now the scream of the jet engines

sounded like banshees. The plane circled once, England, London, the green fields lay below, all she loved lay below. Max with his gentleness, his maturity; she closed her eyes for a moment, the only man she would ever love, had ever loved, the man who held her heart. Once they had been one. Once she had lain safe in his arms in the sure knowledge that he loved her, thinking it would be forever, that nothing would ever come between them.

She turned and looked out of the cabin window. Soon they would reach Berlin. She could hardly see the countryside below for the tears which filled her eyes.

Fumbling, with trembling fingers she drew the postcard from her handbag — the coloured postcard with its picture of Berlin Zoo. Once again she read the words which were already burned into her mind, her heart, her whole being in letters of fire, the words about which she had lied, for indeed the card said *'Wish you were here'* — but the code meant that her mother had not been released from the Eastern sector ... her friends had failed and more than likely been either shot or interned and tortured for what they had tried to do.

Once more she looked out of the window. The sun was setting behind the massing clouds of the coming night — scarlet, blood red ... spilled blood.

The plane started to lose height. She closed her eyes against the coming horror that life held for her behind the Iron Curtain ...

THE END

We do hope that you have enjoyed reading this large print book.

Did you know that all of our titles are available for purchase?

We publish a wide range of high quality large print books including:
Romances, Mysteries, Classics
General Fiction
Non Fiction and Westerns

Special interest titles available in large print are:
The Little Oxford Dictionary
Music Book, Song Book
Hymn Book, Service Book

Also available from us courtesy of Oxford University Press:
Young Readers' Dictionary
(large print edition)
Young Readers' Thesaurus
(large print edition)

For further information or a free brochure, please contact us at:
Ulverscroft Large Print Books Ltd.,
The Green, Bradgate Road, Anstey,
Leicester, LE7 7FU, England.
Tel: (00 44) **0116 236 4325**
Fax: (00 44) **0116 234 0205**

TOO MANY LOVES

Juliet Gray

Justin Caldwell, a famous personality of stage and screen, was blessed with good looks and charm that few women could resist. Stacy was a newcomer to England and she was not impressed by the handsome stranger; she thought him arrogant, ill-mannered and detestable. By the time that Justin desired to begin again on a new footing it was much too late to redeem himself in her eyes, for there had been too many loves in his life.